This *good* Thing

This *good* Thing

JOY E. RANCATORE

LOGOS & MYTHOS PRESS
SLIDELL, LA, USA

For My Sunflower:
May you grow up straight and tall;
May my love cushion each fall;
May your future shine bright
Beneath God's nurturing light.

*Even on the darker days,
we can be thankful for
this good thing—LIFE.*

Other Works

Fiction

Carolina's Legacy Collection:
Any Good Thing: A Novel
This Good Thing: A Novella
Every Good Thing: A Short Story Collection
One Good Thing: An Epistolary

The Crux Anthology
"Ealiverel Awakened"
Edited & Compiled by Rachael Ritchey

Nonfiction

Finders Keepers: A Practical Approach to Find and Keep Your Writing Critique Partner
Joy E. Rancatore and Meagan Smith

Table of Contents

Prologue   1

I   Counting Petals   3

II   Picking Plants   7

Letters for Rachael: When You've Got a Feeling, but You're Unsure Whether or Not to Follow It   19

III   Tilling Soil   23

Letters for Rachael: When You Fall in Love   33

IV   Planting Seeds   39

Letters for Rachael: When You Say "Yes" to a First Date   47

V   Watering Growth   53

Letters for Rachael: When You're Ready to Say "I Do"   57

VI   Pruning Weeds   63

Letters for Rachael: When You Question Your Worth & Wonder How to be a Friend   67

VII   Nurturing Soil   71

Letters for Rachael: ~~When You Face Death~~ When You Embrace Life   81

VIII   Smelling Blossoms   83

Letters for Rachael: When You Become a Mother   89

IX   Gathering Harvest   93

Letters for Rachael: When You Need to Grieve   99

X   Resting Earth   101

Epilogue   103

Prologue

This is a love story.

It's not one love story, though. It's puppy love and forever love. It's mother love and the power of love. It's your loves, my loves and the caliber of love that stares death down and roars, "You cannot quench me!"

It's a love that lasts long past and despite this earth's tragedies. It's an eternal love—a love that defies human comprehension.

Ben and Carolina experienced this mighty love; and it is their tale we follow, interwoven with Carolina's legacy of letters left for their daughter, Rachael, after the too-brief time they shared on earth ... plus one year more.

I

Counting Petals

S he gripped the sides of the bathroom vanity, her knuckles whiter than usual. The crimson-spotted tissue in her left hand held her unseeing gaze as she considered what it could mean. Another cough rose deep within, and she braced herself for its jarring explosion. Once the spasm subsided, she flushed the tissue with its terrifying contents. Out of sight … not out of mind.

She stared ahead, straight into her own eyes. "Windows to the soul," they were labeled. Could she glimpse a lurking enemy within, too, if she looked closely?

Tears welled instead, blurring her vision. She followed the path of a single drop. It trickled toward her jawline, where it hung in a moment of rebellion against gravity's insolent force before vanishing.

A light tap switched her focus to the door behind her. "You ready?"

His voice still stirred butterflies within her. Its softness reassured her, despite looming fears. The intensity of her love coupled with a horror at an imagined existence without his voice. As those feelings collided, her breathing came harder. She closed her eyes and forced herself to breathe, slowly and deeply. One more exhale. No need to keep him worrying.

"Coming!"

She wiped unfallen tears from her freckles and rubbed beneath her emerald eyes, smoothing an attempt at masking the dark circles left by a sleepless night. A quick blow of her nose, a wash of her hands, a tug at her button-up and a final tuck of loose strands of hair before Carolina turned to face her future.

Ben sat on their bed, his smile frayed. He offered his hands to embrace hers. "Pray with me?" With her nod and lowered lashes, he bowed his head.

"Father God, you know we're both scared, uncertain, worried. We pray that you'll give the doctor wisdom. Help him know exactly what's causing Carolina's coughing. We trust you in this and put it in your hands. We pray for healing, for it to be nothing serious; but, God, we know your will is best. Strengthen our faith in whatever lies ahead. In your name we come to you today, Amen."

The mist in their eyes couldn't veil the love that passed between them before Ben pulled his wife into his arms. She rested her cheek on his head as her hair draped his shoulder. They separated and nodded to one another before walking out, hand in hand.

§

Across all medical facilities—doctors' offices, waiting rooms, labs and hospital rooms—exists one unifying factor. It's neither visible nor tangible. Words fumble with its description. Somewhere between a scent and an eerie brush against the veil to another realm, this sense affects all in its reach to some extent.

Some more than others.

As the stiff paper runner of the exam table shifted beneath her, Carolina found herself drenched by this other sense. She shuddered beneath its cascade, simultaneously icy and boiling. Ben half stood, concern hacking trenches along his face as he reached toward his wife.

An abrupt rapping at the door interrupted an assessment of her reaction and shepherded Dr. Clarke's entrance. Tanned from many golf rounds, the general practitioner had grown up in the little town but moved away for school. Bellum, Georgia, had welcomed its golden son back with open arms right after his med school graduation. He inherited his mentor's practice less than a decade and two wives later. While his hair had lightened when he was still in his thirties, it did so gracefully and evenly, leaving him with a distinguished sheen.

"Good morning, Pastor. Carolina." Carl Clarke had been indifferent to religion most of his life, but he found himself drawn to religious women and dutifully attended the church choice of his current wife. Sue Ellen was one of those few front-row Baptists, so her husband had a prime view of Rev. Ben Burns every Sunday morning and most Wednesday evenings.

"I was surprised to see your chart this morning. What seems to be the trouble?"

Carolina subconsciously gripped her husband's hand before launching in to the explanation of what had brought her there.

"Well, I suppose I've felt a little short of breath for a while now—not sure how long. But the cough ... that started a couple months ago. It wasn't so bad at first, but it stuck around and then it started getting worse until ...." A bracing eye-lock with Ben bolstered her strength to finish. "Sunday afternoon, I was weeding one of my flower beds and had a coughing fit. When I pulled my hand away, it was covered in blood."

Dr. Clarke's hand ceased writing, pen straight up, mid-stroke. He absorbed all emotion from his face before lifting it to his patient.

"And since then?"

Her nod barely perceptible, Carolina confirmed, "Every time I cough. Sometimes a little; other times a lot."

"Any tightness in your chest? Changes in your appetite or weight?"

"Tightness, I guess ... but I'm typically anxious this time of year. We have a number of women's events at church. Those always stress me out more than they should. And, I couldn't say about weight. I make it a habit to avoid the scale."

The doctor mirrored her feeble smile before continuing his questions. "Any other unusual aches or pains? Swelling? Anything else out of the ordinary?"

"I always have aches and pains—too much bending over my garden, I guess." Carolina paused to consider his questions and the potential answers. "My joints have been sore more often, I think. Right around my shoulder and even under my arms. I hadn't really thought much about that. Just chalked them up as random pains."

"A couple months back you complained your neck hurt. Remember?" Ben interjected.

"I thought I was getting sick because my glands felt swollen. I didn't get sick and then forgot about it." Her laugh twirled beneath frills of nervousness as symptom after symptom danced across her mind.

Dr. Clarke felt the glands in Carolina's neck and the joints she'd mentioned and continued to give her a thorough exam, all the way down to her reflexes. They laughed as her lower leg shot out and clipped Ben's knee, sinking him to the chair.

Once the exam was done and the doctor sat down, Carolina locked sight lines with him before asking with a statement's inflection, "It's bad, isn't it." The flicker in his returned gaze and pause in his answer confirmed what her senses had warned her earlier.

"I need to run you through a series of tests before I can give you a definite answer." Carolina was no ordinary patient, as Dr. Clarke knew. She raised an invisible armor around herself as she erased any reactions from her face, but she knew. "I think you already have some possibilities in mind. I won't dispel them, but I am intentionally calling them 'possibilities.' Nothing more."

Carolina nodded as she willed the tears to recede. A time would come for them to fall, but she wouldn't let it be yet. She could feel Ben's struggle match hers—each of them striving to make sense of the uncertainty in this new reality.

Dr. Clarke explained each test he was ordering before clicking his pen and picking up his chart. "Wanda will be here in a few minutes to draw some blood, and I should have a schedule of events for you soon after that."

His attempts at humor couldn't overshadow the significance of the speed with which he set her future in motion. As he rose, Carolina rested a hand on the sleeve of his stark white coat. "Wait. Rachael—we need to pick her up from school. I promised we'd shop for a dress for the back-to-school party. It's a big deal—her sixth-grade year and all."

Dr. Clarke flashed his signature dashing smile. "We'll have you done and ready to shop before three."

II

Picking Plants

Ben held Carolina's hand as the nurse drew blood from her veins—bright blue lines scattered across milk-white skin. He considered how many more procedures he'd need to watch her endure and cleared a choking mass from his throat.

He studied Carolina's features—soft, full lips as red as strawberries in early summer; long eyelashes that curled nearly to her arched brows; the button nose he loved to kiss; the face usually beaming with humor and love. Instead, it was strained, stretched. No matter how hard she tried to hide them, Carolina's feelings remained visible to him.

As the exam with Dr. Clarke had unfolded, Ben watched her carousel of emotions. They flashed across her face like a silent horror film.

Fear. Confusion. Uncertainty. Panic. Sorrow. Resignation ... not quite.

Resolve.

The reel stopped as she made her emotional stand.

Ben's internal reactions echoed hers. They struck doubly as he felt both hers and his own—a double-edged sword to his heart. When Carolina mentioned their daughter, Ben lost his breath to the realization that Carolina had accepted the unspoken diagnosis as fact and dropped a heartbeat at a vision of Rachael and what the test results could mean for their family.

His gaze shifted next to the hand in her lap. As usual, it twisted and turned, tightening and loosening—more than usual, since the nurse held her other hand captive. A smile brushed his lips as he thought of how she never could be still. He pictured her Bible in them. Even in her daily quiet time, her fingers guided her eyes as she felt the words lining the thin pages. He often teased her that she would rub off the words.

He reached for her hands as they waited for the next test. He raised her knuckles to his lips. Their eyes locked, and volumes passed.

"We will fight this—together. Whatever it is." Her uncertain smile with its translucent armor of determination shot a pang of grief through him. He'd been in the dark alley between families and doctors for enough years to know what awaited them wasn't slight.

The remainder of the morning and early afternoon spun around them, a revolving door of medical personnel, procedure rooms, machines and tests. Ben witnessed the energy drain out of his wife as the day progressed. After the final test, he took her hand for the stroll to their Bronco.

They had been elated the previous month when he wrote their final check for it. The whole family had celebrated by putting the back seats down and sitting there, gazing across the lake and up at the stars. They had feasted on a picnic of Carolina's homemade bread, spread with cinnamon butter Rachael had made. They saw a shooting star that night, and each one made a wish. His had been for countless more nights like that one.

Ben considered his wife's face again and said, "You know, you could wait until tomorrow to take Rach shopping." He knew what her response would be but had to suggest an alternative when he saw the fatigue blanketing her face.

Carolina's smile warmed his heart as she squeezed his hand. "I told her today, and today it will be."

As Ben drove toward the front of the upper elementary school, a giant banner flapped in the light September breeze.

Back-to-School Bash
Sponsored by the Class of 2002

Bellum's traditions set everyone's social calendar. This bash always topped the list for fifth and sixth graders in the rural town, and the sixth graders took their role as party planners seriously. Surrounded by a group of friends, Rachael stood under the sign she had helped paint.

Ben chuckled. "Always the life of the party, isn't she?"

"She's been a social butterfly since she was a baby. Remember in the church nursery? The workers couldn't put her down unless she was surrounded by at least three other babies." Carolina's cheeks flushed with the memory.

Ben noticed the one boy in the circle. He stood next to Rachael as he told the group a story, complete with hand motions that clearly mimed something football-related. All the girls laughed when he finished, but Rachael grabbed his arm as she doubled over. Her bright red ponytail flipped over her head and brushed the ground with its length. Ben knew how her laugh sounded—*elflike* is how he described it. Just like her mother's.

He watched the boy take his little girl's hand as they continued to share the joke. He worried about the way Rachael looked with her deep blue eyes at that boy. His concern came from where he'd seen the same look—in Carolina's eyes twenty-five years earlier. He had seen it that first day they met—the day after Labor Day. The biggest problem was Ben saw a lot of himself in this kid, Jack. Heaven knows Ben put Carolina through far too much, and he did not want his princess to face the same.

His sigh attracted Carolina's gaze. She laughed. "Stop worrying about those two. You know Rachael got the same ability to read people that I have."

"That's what worries me. I was a train wreck."

Carolina leaned over to plant a kiss on his cheek and whisper, "But look at you now."

He cupped her chin and said, "Because of you." After kissing the tip of his wife's nose, he added another point to his argument. "Plus, he looks like he's up to no good. Perhaps I should ask his intentions."

His wife shook her head. "You're really too much. You spent most of the summer playing catch with him in our backyard. Let those babies be. Besides, would it be the worst thing in the world if one day—many years from now—those two decide they love each other? They have known each other since birth."

Ben narrowed his eyes in his wife's direction. "I still don't have to like the idea. And, they've been doing an awful lot of growing up over the past few weeks."

"Well, you're right about that." Carolina sighed as Ben drove alongside the group of preteens. Rachael waved to her parents before turning to give hugs to two of her friends—one of which was Jack, Ben noticed.

"Hey, Sunflower! Ready to go shopping?" Carolina turned to accept a quick hug and peck on the cheek from her bubbly daughter.

"Totally! Anna Claire said she saw a bunch of super cute dresses at Apple Blossoms. Could we start there?"

"Driver?" Carolina teased.

"Certainly, Ma'am. Miss." Ben tipped his head toward each of his girls but couldn't maintain a straight face as he played along.

One benefit of a small town—it didn't take more than a few minutes to get anywhere. Before Rachael had finished telling her parents how one of the snobby girls in her class ended up with a tray full of ketchup-covered food all over her new dress, Ben pulled up to the door of one of Bellum's two clothing stores. He hopped out and opened the ladies' doors simultaneously, earning an eye roll from his wife and a giggle from his daughter.

"Your chariot will return in one hour, m'ladies." Ben left them with a dramatic bow before returning to his seat. He gripped the steering wheel and blinked back a creeping fog as he watched the love of his life smile and laugh with their daughter. Unanswered What Ifs flitted through his mind as he eased away from the curb. He may not get feelings like his wife did, but he'd become adept at reading them on her face and interpreting their messages. He knew they both believed the diagnosis would be grim. He thought about how their faith would be tested and sent a plea for strength heavenward.

§

While Ben visited church members, Rachael enjoyed her shopping spree with her mom. Age eleven seemed to be a growing year, judging by the high-water jeans that had covered her shoes a mere three months earlier. As she looked down at the new jeans, Rachael contemplated how quickly things could change. Three months—two sizes. One more year—junior high. She was beginning to understand why adults always talked about time flying.

They chose some more jeans and a pair of khakis for the school year. Finally, they got to the dresses. Two armfuls later, the mother-daughter duo bustled back into the dressing room. Carolina pulled off the sweater she frequently wore on car rides or in chilly stores.

Rachael's gaze latched onto the bandage affixed to the inside of her mother's arm. She had her suspicions about this appointment. Her mother rarely had to go to the doctor, and she could tell her parents were anxious. During their family worship time that week, her dad had prayed for God to help the doctors figure out why the coughing had gotten worse. Being a PK—a preacher's kid—Rachael had overheard dozens of grown-up conversations in people's homes or hospital rooms as her dad listened to their diagnoses ... and the resulting prognoses. She knew tense, drawn faces typically meant the patient's future would be short.

Rachael studied her mother's face and saw an exhaustion and a worry she hadn't noticed before. "You went to the doctor today. How'd it go?"

Her mother's smile lacked its typical warmth and depth and didn't comfort her. "Dr. Clarke was super thorough. I think he ran every test our hospital offers." Her joke punched Rachael in the gut. She knew no doctor ran that many tests without reason.

"Did they find out what's wrong?" Rachael asked the question, though she wasn't sure she wanted an answer.

Carolina shook her head and smiled. "These things take time, Sunflower."

Despite her concern, Rachael grinned at her mom's nickname for her. She'd heard the story behind it often enough to wonder if she actually remembered the day she, as a curious three-year-old, discovered the wonder of sunflowers. Her mother had been in the garden all day. Rachael was with her, running along the paths around each mound of growth or digging with her miniature trowel.

She had stopped several times to gently stroke the yellow petals as they bent toward her. This time she passed beneath them was different. The flowers didn't greet her.

"Mama, come see!" Rachael led her mother to see what she'd discovered, pulling on her fingers with all her might, until they stood before a line of bright yellow blooms. Carolina's laugh had made her daughter giggle, and she picked Rachael up to see the cheerful tops of the flowers.

"These are sunflowers. They're very special because they love light so much, they follow it!" Carolina pointed to the light above them as she moved her arm in imitation of the path she described. "As the sun moves across our sky during the day, these flowers will follow after it."

Rachael's widened eyes took in the fascinating world above and around and beneath her. "Sunflowers love light," she whispered in awe before making an announcement. "I love light, too!"

"The sun reminds me of God. When we follow him—just like these flowers follow the sun—we will grow brighter as we get taller and stronger. We can share our cheerfulness and, one day, spread seeds to others." Mother and daughter smiled at one another as Carolina made a comparison beyond the total comprehension of a toddler. She liked to plant seeds in her little one that would one day produce an eternal harvest.

Rachael had moved tiny fingers from petting the silky petals to frame her mother's face as the garden-inspired life lesson continued. "You can be just like these sunflowers, my little one. As you grow up, tall and strong, keep your face toward God's light so you reflect his brightness on those around you. Share his truth and good news by spreading the seeds of his gospel. God will use you in such amazing ways, my little sunflower."

Carolina kissed her daughter's cheek before Rachael wiggled down from her mother's arms. She ran around in circles, arms outstretched and face lifted toward the warmth of the sun. "I'm a sunflower, mama!"

"Try on this emerald green one. It'll look perfect with your hair and skin tone." At the sound of her mother's voice, Rachael's focus returned to the dressing room.

She rested a hand on her hip as she contemplated her image in the mirror. "You mean fire and ice?" She scrunched up her nose and frowned at what she considered detriments to her appearance.

Her mother leaned beside her as they looked at each other's reflections. A smile of satisfaction spread across her face. "What a beautiful description." She laughed as Rachael rolled her eyes. "One day you'll learn to embrace this body God gave you as what it is—designed by a Creator who's perfect and makes all things beautiful in His way."

Rachael looked again at the mother she thought was one of the loveliest women she'd ever seen. They did look almost identical. Maybe red hair and pale skin weren't the worst things in the world.

"Mama?" Rachael faced her mother. "Please don't keep anything from me. I want to know what the tests say. Okay?"

She noticed a flicker of something she couldn't quite label in her mother's expression but also saw the honesty when, after a moment's pause, Carolina nodded slightly. "Okay."

Rachael grinned and spun around to snatch the emerald dress from its hanger. A shimmy, two slips and a zip later, she twirled in front of the mirror as the full skirt billowed around her and the gem-studded straps shimmered under the fluorescent lighting. The brightness of her smile made it clear all the other dresses would be returning to the racks.

"Like it was made for you," Carolina whispered, beaming at her daughter.

"Jack's silver tie will look good with these straps, too, for when we have pictures made." At her mother's raised eyebrow, Rachael quickly added, "It's not a date. We know we're too young to date. We're just such good friends and we promised to dance together because it would be weird with anyone else."

"I know you two have a special bond. I went into labor with you the day after my first visit with Becky and little Jack; well, not the first visit, but the first one he was actually awake. He was squealing and squirming, and you started kicking. I think you decided he'd make a good playmate, and you were ready to come out and join him." Carolina tucked a loose strand of hair behind her daughter's ear. "Your bond has only grown as you two have gotten older. And, I know what that can feel like, even when you're young. I fell in love with your daddy when we were fifteen."

"Really?" Her smile fanned across her face. She knew her parents had just celebrated twenty-five years of love, but she hadn't thought to do the math.

"Really. It was love at first sight. I'll tell you about it …," a cloud passed Carolina's face as she inhaled before continuing, "… one day. Let's get this dress off and check out; what do you say?"

Rachael hadn't missed her mother's pause, but she also recognized this wasn't an afternoon for worry. "Sounds awesome. You think we could talk Daddy into ice cream?"

"Does that man ever need convincing when ice cream's involved?" Carolina's laughter echoed in the small space.

As the two stumbled out of the dressing room—their arms full of fabric—they heard a familiar chuckle.

"I see you're buying out the store. Can't leave you ladies alone when shopping's involved." Ben stood, hands on hips, an unconvincing image of disapproval.

Rachael dropped her load of unneeded dresses on a chair before holding up the green dress and swaying with it fanned out before her. "This is the one, Daddy. What do you think?"

"Well, I happen to be partial to that color. It matches my best girl's eyes." He winked at his wife before adding, "And I know it will look perfect on my princess."

Rachael ran to her father, throwing her arms around his neck and planting a kiss on his cheek. "I think this calls for ice cream," she whispered in his ear.

His answering belly laugh threw both ladies into a fit of giggles. While Carolina paid for the new wardrobe items, Ben and Rachael helped one of the sales ladies hang up all the other dresses.

The trio left the store, bags in tow, as they discussed which flavors they would choose and agreed that waffle cones were a given.

§

That night Ben slid into bed beside his wife, pulling her into his arms. She rested her head on his shoulder as they discussed the day's events.

"Mary from Dr. Clarke's office called. They expect to have all the results Monday, so she went ahead and made me an appointment for 10:00." Ben noticed his wife's pause and the concern weighing down her voice when she continued. "She also told me to block off some extra time because Dr. Clarke may want to run more tests."

Ben pressed his face into Carolina's hair and breathed her in. He could feel her fear and longed to tell her it would all be okay. They had a full weekend of blissful ignorance ahead of them. He resolved to do the one thing he could and make it the best for them. "How do you want to spend our weekend?"

His gentle whisper in her ear drew a smile to the corners of her mouth. She turned until she could look at him. "With you and with our girl."

He returned her grin and brushed a kiss across her forehead. "Should I get someone to preach for me? Do you want to take a trip?"

Her lyrical laughter filled him with the warming glow only she could produce in him. "No, silly. I want to do ordinary activities with my two extraordinary loves. Tomorrow, I want to fix my little girl's hair and help her with her dress and take tons of obnoxious mom pictures of her with her friends. Saturday, I want us to eat breakfast in the garden and have a picnic lunch by the lake. I want to cook all your favorite foods tomorrow night. I want to laugh and sing and dance in the kitchen with you. I want to keep Rachael up past her bedtime for a cheesy movie and popcorn and I want to fall asleep in your arms. I want us to go to church together on Sunday like we always do. I want to hear you share and explain God's word in that beautiful way you do. I want to sing all my favorite hymns with the beautiful family—and church family—God gave me. And then, in the afternoon, I want to rest in the shade of our pines, all piled up in the hammock together. I want to live life with you both, squeeze every beautiful second out of it that I can and soak them in until they overflow. That's how I want to spend our weekend."

Foreheads together, they spoke about all the everyday things they loved to share. Ben wrapped his wife in his arms as she laid her head on his chest.

"Ben?"

He heard the tone in his wife's voice shift to seriousness. "Mm-hmmm," he responded against her temple.

"Whatever it is—whatever the diagnosis—we need to tell Rachael. I don't want to keep the truth from her and pretend everything's okay if it's not." Carolina tilted her head back to look up at him. "She'll know anyway."

Ben sighed. "Dang kid's as intuitive as her mother." Their smiles matched before he continued. "And, of course you're right ... as usual. I can hear her serious little voice saying, 'We're all in this together, guys.'"

Carolina laughed at his spot-on impression of their daughter before turning somber once more. She settled back against Ben. "It struck me today just how much I still have to teach her—about growing up, being a woman of God ... so many things. I don't want to leave any of those important things unsaid."

Ben kissed her head and fought to swallow the growing lump in his throat. Long after his wife fell asleep, he remained awake. He worried and raged until he cried and prayed. Birdsong twittered around the couple when he finally succumbed to the steadiness of Carolina's breathing and drifted off to sleep.

§

The family had what Rachael would call a "happily-ever-after" weekend. Ben frequently caught himself stopping to watch his two girls. When they smiled and laughed at each other, it was as though a mirror had found a way to live.

Though none of them spoke of Monday morning, they all felt its presence inching ever closer. It was the darkness lingering on the edges of their shiny memory-making moments. When they dropped Rachael off at school that Monday morning, Ben recognized a young girl's terror mostly covered by her desire to be strong. He noted the extra seconds in the hug she gave her mother and continued the prayer he'd started when Carolina showed him her final symptom.

After an impromptu date by the lake, Ben and Carolina went to her appointment at Bellum Medical Hospital. This time, the receptionist led them into Dr. Clarke's office. As the couple waited next to each other, they spied a large envelope covering much of the desk in front of them. The truth it contained filled the room. Ben discovered breathing had become a challenging task.

"Good morning." Dr. Clarke whisked in, shaking their hands before sitting down behind his desk.

Ben noticed the absence of light in the doctor's smile and his careful avoidance of the package in front of him. The room's stillness expanded until it pressed down on them. In the unsettling quiet he thought he heard Carolina's heartbeat. Perhaps it was his. Either way, its pulse reverberated so loudly he struggled to hear the doctor's words.

"I've known you both long enough to get to the point." Dr. Clarke leaned forward, strategically placing his arms around the packet of scans and other results. He took a deep breath as he twisted his wedding band, before directly addressing his patient.

"Carolina, your tests are suspicious of metastatic breast cancer. We'll need a biopsy to present a definitive diagnosis. The CT scan showed spots on your right breast, lymph nodes and both lungs. It appears to have spread to your bones as well, but we need further testing to confirm that as well. I've ordered a bone scan for you today and the biopsy first thing tomorrow."

"How long?" Her breathless question, forced from her ravaged body, sliced like an arrow through Ben's heart.

Dr. Clarke, too, flinched at her matter-of-fact question. His voice lowered to a tone he rarely used. "I'll be honest, we may not hit a year; however, we can fight this. There are treatment options, and miracles exist. We can't predict them or even explain them—with science, anyway—but they do happen, as you two know."

Carolina's grip tightened on Ben's hand.

"I've already been in touch with Dr. Jay Kumari, the best oncologist I know in Atlanta; and he's requested this further testing. You will be in great hands with him. If it works for you, we've got an appointment for you Friday in Atlanta. He will have all the test results from us then and will have a treatment plan ready to propose to you. If the tests confirm our suspicions, Dr. K will want to administer the first treatment early next week."

A small sound escaped Carolina's mouth. She closed and then reopened it, continuing slowly as if weighing each word before releasing it. "If it's not a cure, why attempt treatments?"

Dr. Clarke's face softened as his eyes rested on the envelope. "Carolina, this is your choice. I'm not going to pretend there's a rosy picture to be found in this mess. And, you're right, with cancer of this type and at this stage, we don't expect to cure it but we can treat it. Sometimes that gives us months or even a year; but, every now and then, we get a miracle. Dr. Kumari aims for the miracles. As your doctor—and your friend—I would urge you to meet with him and follow whatever plan he sets up for you. Let's at least try."

Ben found himself engulfed by a vice-like pressure as the news coiled around him. He heard the plea in the doctor's final sentence and glimpsed a fleeting flash of hope in Carolina's eyes. The doctor's next words came more clearly to his ears.

"With cancer, especially this advanced, you as the patient call the shots. Your doctors will give you some plays to choose from; but, if the treatments get too rough and they don't seem to be helping, you decide whether to try a different plan ... or whether to call it."

Carolina pressed back into her chair as Ben watched her struggle to process the previous five minutes.

"I've thrown a heckuva lot at you guys. Would you like me to give you some time here before we talk more about appointments and tests?"

Ben saw Carolina's slight head movement and spoke for her. "Please, doc." As the physician rose and crossed to his door, Ben added, "And, thanks."

He studied his wife's profile. She stared straight ahead as though she could glimpse her future in the diplomas hanging on the wall. He felt her struggle—fear, sorrow, worry, uncertainty, disbelief and finally, once more ... resolve. He knew she'd made a decision before she turned to him with the hint of a smile.

"I'm ready to fight this for you and for Rachael. I will pray for a super miracle—that there's some mistake or it all goes away—but I'm also realistic and understand these failing bodies we've got." Carolina's hand moved from Ben's hand to his cheek, brushing a tear away with her thumb. "I'm praying most for one more year … with you."

"Plus, I need time to write some letters to Rachael—for when she's older. There are certain times in a girl's life when she needs words from her mama. I want to make sure she has them."

Ben studied his wife's face again. He mentally traced a heart freckle-to-freckle around her cheeks and nose as he felt the ache of how much he loved the woman before him and how impossible it was for him to imagine life without her brightening its days.

He covered her hand with his and gave her his best effort at a smile before responding, "A quarter of a century of knowing—and loving—you is nowhere near enough. We'll fight to make it twenty-five, plus one year more."

Letters for Rachael

When You've Got a Feeling, but You're Unsure Whether or Not to Follow It

My precious Rachael,

We have so much in common, it's sometimes scary. I believe those similarities dive far deeper than our sunburn-prone skin.

Embrace those tingles you get, baby girl. I have had the same types of feelings since I was your age. Intuition is the best word to describe it, I think. Pretty much without fail I have regretted every time I haven't listened to mine.

We started talking about this last week. You told me about the feelings you had about your friend Beth and her family—how you felt like something was really wrong the week of July 4 and you turned out to be right. They ended up in the hospital with her dad's heart attack when they should have been on vacation. I told you then I have similar feelings about things and people; but the phone rang, and I never finished sharing about my experiences and what I've learned about them over the years. So, here you go:

I suppose the first time I consciously chose to ignore a feeling, I wasn't much older than you. Oh, I'd had this intuition way before I'd ever heard that word, but this was the first time I recognized a feeling for exactly what it was but decided to do my own thing anyway.

It was my seventh-grade year, and we had a new girl join us three weeks after school started. Pamela had long, dark hair. It was super straight, and I thought it was the prettiest hair I'd ever seen. (See, I wasn't a fan of my red hair back then either. That's why I told you you'd grow out of your loathing of your features—I did.)

Anyway, she didn't smile much, wore long sleeves all the time and kept to herself. I decided we needed to be friends, so I introduced myself. I walked right up after her first day, stuck my hand out to shake hers and said, "Hi! I'm Carolina, and I'd love to be your friend."

She reluctantly took my hand and, when she did, I had the strongest feeling I'd ever experienced. I felt pain and fear. It was horrible and oh so dark. All I wanted to do was run far, far away. I didn't, though—not yet anyway.

We were friends, but I didn't let myself get too close. I pulled her into my group of friends and slowly spiraled back from her until I sometimes went a couple days without even speaking to her. But, sometimes, I would steal a glance at her. I could see how unhappy she was and, every time, there was that feeling, like it was radiating off of her and casting its gloomy rays over me.

One Friday we walked up to the bathroom sinks to wash our hands at the same time. Out of habit, she rolled up her long sleeves until I gasped. Both arms were covered with cuts, scratches and bruises. I'll never forget the look on Pamela's face. It was a mashup of surprise, embarrassment and—primarily—fear. No—not fear. Terror. She was absolutely terrified of something ... or someone. Before I could do anything but stare open-mouthed, she tugged both sleeves down and tucked them firmly in her palms before rushing out the door.

I never saw her again.

All weekend I wrestled with how I should tell someone what I saw, how I should have said something, how I should do something. Monday morning I decided to find Pamela before homeroom and find out what was going on.

I couldn't find her. The day went on, and I still didn't see her. None of our other friends had seen her either. I finally had her homeroom teacher and asked her where Pamela was. She said she hadn't come to school that morning. I saw a worried look on her face, and she asked if I knew where she could be. That feeling rose again and urged me to tell her what I'd seen. Instead, I ran from it again and just shook my head.

The following week I overheard my parents talking about how awful it was that little Pamela had been taken and her parents put in jail. Piecing together stolen fragments of conversations and the gossip I believed, I figured out she had been sent to another state for foster care. I cried myself to sleep for months after that because I had known—but I didn't do anything.

From then on, I listened to my instincts. Some great things have come from that. Your father was one. You were another.

The moment I met your father, I knew he was special. He had a great purpose ahead of him, and I thought I may be part of it. I'll tell you our whole story in another letter.

On to you, my precious sunflower, I longed for and prayed for a child for years. I thought I was pregnant at least a dozen times, but every time ended the same and each time hurt more than the last. We decided to move to Bellum about a year before you were born. It didn't take me long to discover our lake. You know how much I love going there; it may not be set against my mountains in Idaho, but it's still a special piece of nature that speaks to me. On one of my daily walks around it, I rested for a while on a bench. The sun was starting to fade. I had been praying about this strange new place and my desire for a child and so much more as I walked, so it seemed fitting to close my eyes and lift my face toward the setting sun as I breathed an amen.

With that simple word, warmth spread through me, peace washed over me and my intuition kicked in. I knew I would hold a baby girl in my arms soon. I flew home on the wings of my heart that day.

Most of my feelings about things are far less dramatic and life-changing. I always listen, though. At least, until a couple months ago. I began having this physical ... something. Honestly, I don't have a word for it. It wasn't an ache or pain and didn't live in any specific region of my body. There was nothing I could describe to a doctor as an actual symptom—it was just something.

Accompanying this enigma was a feeling—a bad one. I knew then that something was wrong with me, but I couldn't figure out how to request a doctor's appointment for a feeling and a ... something.

I should have listened; though I'm not sure my story would have ended any differently. I think God was simply preparing me for this rocky journey.

As your own warnings or feelings pop up through your life, I urge you to listen. If you're unsure if it's real or your fickle emotions playing tricks on you—or the sixth piece of pizza you ate too late the night before— use wisdom. God's word will guide you to truth and surety as you seek to understand this gift God has given us.

III

Tilling Soil

Monday and Tuesday continued for Carolina in a whirlwind of waiting and lying still and being poked and prodded. Wednesday, she felt numb as reality pressed heavy on her heart but her brain couldn't quite comprehend its meaning. Thursday, they packed for what they chose to make an impromptu family vacation.

In the hotel room that evening, Carolina rested her head, eyes closed, on the wingback chair. The week had left its mark. Her temples throbbed. Her shoulders sagged beneath the tension dropped on them by worry for what lay ahead. And, she was tired—as she had been for months. If she'd only gone to the doctor sooner ...

She shook her head. That line of thinking would do no good. She could have rushed to Dr. Clarke with a dozen random issues over the past six months. Every mother on the planet goes through seasons of exhaustion. Every gardener experiences joint pain, aches, stiffness. No, all she could do was look forward. Looking back wouldn't help anyone.

Carolina had watched the cancer war in others over the years. She pictured the pale, gaunt faces of so many—Megan, Justin, Anita, Tom. Life drained from faces. Beautiful hair fell away. Strength failed.

Could hers hold?

Father, give me strength.

Four small words sent a shot of peace coursing through her system. The weight rose from her shoulders; the throbbing ceased.

Loved voices reached through her reverie. "What do you want to do while we're here?" Ben was asking Rachael while they unpacked.

Her grin turned mischievous as she clarified, "Anything?" She had the ability to make her parents laugh long and hard with a simple well-timed word. This time, it was the medicine Carolina needed. Her mirth prompted Rachael to sit in her lap.

"Within reason." Ben countered their daughter's request.

Rachael presented her wishes.

"A Braves game is a given."

"Of course," he agreed.

"Most important, I want to spend as much time as possible with you two …" Rachael added a dramatic pause. "… in that awesome pool we passed on the way in." Her impish grin shone, and they decided to try it out before supper.

§

The next morning, Dr. Kumari confirmed Dr. Clarke's suspicions and then introduced his treatment plan for Carolina. He would start her on chemotherapy treatments the following Tuesday. She would have three more treatments, one every three weeks. She was encouraged to hear that she wouldn't have to stay in the hospital after each one—unless she had complications, of course. Since hers was an advanced cancer, they would re-scan her at the end of four treatments and discuss the next steps.

As she leaned against the wall of the elevator in the cancer center, Carolina focused on breathing deeply. She filled her diseased lungs and released her breath reluctantly. She knew the side effects. She knew the ultimate outcome.

One more deep breath.

Ben and Rachael watched her, worry highlighting their faces. She smiled and took their hands. Carolina also knew she loved them and wanted nothing more than to enjoy all the time she could with them. That's where she chose to place her focus.

The family spent most of the weekend in the pool before heading to the Atlanta-Fulton County Stadium on Monday night to watch the first of a four-game series against the Mets. They joined in the tomahawk chop and "Take Me Out to the Ballgame," enjoyed hot dogs and peanuts—as any good baseball fan would do—and cheered their team to victory. All of Atlanta buzzed with chatter about the upcoming playoffs and the Braves' chances.

Carolina slept well Monday night despite the looming threat of the chemicals that would soon invade her system. The weekend had been full and exhausting, but she soaked up the shining rays of each laugh, smile and glance from her husband and daughter. They left a glow on her that the nurses noticed when she arrived at the center Tuesday morning.

"If I hadn't seen your scans, honey, I wouldn't have thought you had a thing in the world wrong with you. You're shining with life." The nurse helped Carolina prepare for her first treatment.

Carolina turned her vibrant smile toward the woman. "My hubby and baby girl have that effect."

She saw a veil of concern slip over the nurse's face and asked, "This is going to get rough, isn't it?"

The nurse's smile faded, and she gripped her patient's hand before answering candidly, "I'm not sure that lovely glow of yours will survive."

Carolina nodded. "That's what I figured." Ben and Rachael appeared, framed in the door's square window. They waved at her and tossed some thumbs up for support. She waved back and laughed as they made silly faces. "I'm fighting for them. For a little more time ... with them."

Dr. Kumari knocked before joining the two women. Carolina greeted him with a smile that felt worn around the edges and devoid of her full heart. "Dr. K, I want to talk to you while my husband and daughter aren't here. I know this plan is for more time ... at best. Of course we pray for miracles, but we also face the probable. I'm in this to fight, but when the treatments' detriments overshadow the benefits, I'm done. I want as much time as I can have with my family, but spending that precious time in torture isn't what I have in mind."

His soft, brown eyes assured Carolina that he understood. "I agree. We will work together on this. I cannot promise any outcomes or timelines, but I can promise to listen to you."

"That's the best promise you can ever make to your patients." With Carolina's nod, her treatments began.

§

Chemo washed away her glow quicker than expected. The combination of a mild reaction around the injection site on her arm and an elevated temperature kept her under watch longer than usual. When violent bouts of vomiting began, her nurse returned with IV fluids and an order from the doctor to admit her for the night.

Carolina preferred the frigid tile surrounding the toilet to hovering over a bucket in her bed. She heaved once more, releasing nothing but her resolve to fight this impossible battle. She felt Ben's hands, gentle on her back. As she pushed herself back into him, he slid his arms around her, pulling her against him to cradle her and the burden she bore. Her tears fell then, a silent acknowledgement of the loss and hurt and the overwhelming feeling of all the treatments still to come.

Once empty of any fluids that could wish to escape the chemicals within her, Carolina found herself more exhausted than she'd ever been. Ben laid her in the hospital bed and lay beside her, gently stroking her arm.

"Take Rach to the game. Please." Her eyelids fell lower, lower. Before she sank into the sweet arms of sleep, she added, "For me."

Ben pressed a kiss to his wife's forehead before lowering his cheek to rest there instead. A tear escaped as he sat up. He brushed it from her cheek and softly kissed her lips. "For you."

§

The Braves' losses over the next two nights did nothing to improve Ben or Rachael's dampened spirits. Watching the woman he loved being tortured from the inside out proved a harder task than Ben had been prepared to undertake. After the second loss, Ben held his daughter's hand as they left the stadium. The oppressive summer heat that clung to everyone and everything in the Southern United States pressed on them from every side. Even the parking lot retained the day's heat, shooting it upward through the soles of their sandals. The outside heat mixed with the emotions within them until every feeling inside melted into part of the whole boiling mess.

"I don't want to do this, Daddy." Rachael's misty voice blasted through the sounds of rowdy fans, honking horns and busy traffic all around. He looked down at her damp face. "I don't want to watch Mama hurt like this. They have to have a better way. They're doctors. Aren't they supposed to heal, not make their patients hurt more?"

"Oh, Chickadee …." Ben scooped his daughter into his arms where she sobbed against his shoulder as he wept inwardly. Her sorrow made his own feel like lava building up, seeking an escape. He calmed himself by stroking her hair and kissing her head until she had released all the pain she could.

Once they'd buckled up to return to the hotel, he lifted her hand in his and turned to face the little girl who would face the demon of death far sooner than any of them had ever imagined. "As horrific as these drugs are on your mother's body, they're also attacking those cancer cells. It doesn't seem right, but this is what doctors have to fight with."

"It seems like some Sci-Fi nightmare. I want it to go away; to be just a horrible dream." Rachael raised glassy eyes to her father. "Mama's so brave. I don't know how she's doing this."

"I don't either. And, she certainly is." Ben smiled as he cupped his daughter's chin. "So are you. Watching your mom going through this has to be terrifying, but you sat by her side all day, hugging her, loving her, getting her more ice chips every time she needed them. When she was sick, she could hear you praying for her. You have no idea how much strength that gave her."

Rachael returned his smile as a glimmer of the usual light reappeared in her eyes. Ben continued, "Baby girl, you don't have to always be strong to be brave. It's sometimes in our weakness when we're the bravest. It's brave to cry. It's brave to ask questions. Your mother and I won't always look brave either. This is going to be hard for all of us. We're all scared and sad and sometimes even angry. We'll have to look out for each other … and might need to take turns being strong."

She nodded and smiled wider. "I may not be strong all the time, but I can be some of the time."

As Rachael threw her arms around her father's neck, he felt a knot lodge in his throat as he choked back a sob. "Me too, Chickadee. Me too."

The next night was a good one. Carolina's violent reactions had ceased. Her medical team had kept her well-hydrated; and, though weak, she was able to return to the hotel where the three of them watched the game on TV and cheered as their team won. Love and joy overpowered their fears and uncertainties as Rachael jumped up and down on her bed like the carefree child she should be. Ben and Carolina shook their heads and laughed as their excitement resulted in happy tears—small moments that sealed big memories away for darker days to come.

§

Carolina's best friend, Becky, arrived for a girls' night the Friday after her first treatment. The two women and Rachael crowded in the bathroom to fix each other's hair and talk and laugh.

"Just promise me you won't give me a mean nickname," Carolina teased her friend.

"Like what?" Becky asked.

"Oh, I don't know … Shiny? Billiard Ball?"

"Daddy Warbucks?" piped up Rachael.

"Hey now!" Carolina grabbed her daughter around her waist in a tickle hug.

"Looks like I'm not the one you have to worry about." Becky laughed.

Carolina sobered as she brushed her daughter's hair, the same color and length as hers. "As long as you let me brush and braid your hair, Rach, I won't mind so much losing mine."

Rachael returned her mother's thin smile before kissing her cheek and whispering, "You got it."

Becky slid a clip into her friend's hair and then quickly wiped away a stray tear. "Have you thought more about shaving it now?"

"Yeah. I think I'll wait. There is a chance it won't make my hair fall out." Carolina laughed as she added, "I mean, it's something like two million to one, but hey! Someone's gotta' be the one, right?"

Ben walked in as the ladies shared another laugh. "Are y'all going to hang out in the bathroom all night or actually go out?"

"We're going! We're going!" Carolina playfully punched her husband's arm on her way out the door. "It sounds like you want us out of here."

"Well, as a matter of fact, I've got a date with this little Missy. I've got big plans to finally defeat her at Chinese checkers."

"Good luck with that, Daddy. You know you've never beat me, right?" Rachael stood, hands on hips, facing down her opponent with the absolute confidence of an eleven-year-old.

"Oh! Look out there!" Becky laughed as she hugged Rachael on her way to the door. "Good luck, Ben. Sounds like you're gonna need it."

"Have fun, you two!" Carolina kissed her husband and daughter. "I love you both."

Those four simple, often mindlessly shared words hung on Carolina's tongue and echoed in her mind as she followed her friend to the car. No longer were those words mere sentiments tossed in passing. They held a lifetime of love in every utterance.

The next day, Carolina uncovered her next challenge. Sores formed inside her mouth. She thought fondly of the fried catfish and hush puppies dipped in cheese sauce she'd enjoyed the night before at Memaw's. Those weren't foods she'd get to enjoy again any time soon, it seemed.

Carolina sighed. She had known this was a possible side effect. One more hurdle to overcome. As the weeks passed, the sores spread inside her mouth and to her lips. She learned the importance of small smiles, tiny bites and cool shakes.

The worst part of all, though, was her inability to kiss her husband and daughter. She resented losing that small privilege she realized she'd taken for granted over the years.

§

Carolina's second treatment went better than the first, and she was able to make it a day trip to Atlanta instead of being hospitalized. In addition to the sores and pains in her arms and legs, she battled occasional stomach cramps. Each Friday, she had blood drawn at the hospital in Bellum, and Dr. Clarke would check in on her. She appreciated his kindness and had noticed at church how he kept an arm around his wife during services and held her hand as they walked down the aisle. As awful as the physical side effects of Carolina's disease were, she also experienced positive results—like the special times she'd been spending with Ben and Rachael and the doctor's attentiveness toward his wife.

The week after her second chemo infusion, Carolina found herself doubled over with the pain of a stomach cramp more intense than any she could recall. As the pain subsided and she slowly straightened, she pushed her hair back from her face and felt before she saw the clump of hair hanging detached in her hand.

Her first urge was to laugh, but her recovering stomach muscles protested. Instead she welcomed a silent stream of tears as she walked to where Ben stood in the kitchen. She held her hand toward him. He understood.

Ben put his arm around her and led her back to the bathroom where he set up his electric razor. Her tears fell in twin waterfalls, watering the silky, vibrant red hair scattered on the tiles beneath her chair. At the end, Ben turned his wife to face him. She saw the moisture on his lashes, the sorrow etched beneath his smile and the ever-present gleam of his love for her in his eyes. His hands cradled her cheeks as he whispered, "I love you more today than yesterday, my beautiful bride." With that declaration, he kissed his wife's bald head.

Temples together, he held her until her broken voice broke the stillness.

"Thank you."

Ben lifted her chin in his fingers, kissed her head again and then pulled a gift box from the cabinet.

"This is from Becky and Rachael," he answered her unspoken question.

Carolina tugged the bow, then ran a finger inside the seams of the wrapping paper. She lifted the lid of the white box and smoothed back the tissue paper inside to reveal a silky, bright red scarf. She raised a shaking hand toward her cracked, trembling lips as the floodgates on her emotion reopened.

"Want me to put it on?" Carolina raised an eyebrow to express her skepticism at Ben's offer. His laughter revealed he had, once again, read her thoughts. "Becky showed me how. Rachael was a willing mannequin."

As Ben lifted the scarf and prepared it for her, Carolina turned toward the mirror for the first time. A sunken face stared back at her— a spectre of her living self. Gone was the hair she had loathed as a self-conscious pre-teen but grew to love as she understood her Creator. No more were the fiery locks her husband passionately ran his fingers through. Lost were the thick strands her baby girl once clutched possessively in her tiny fists. Lost was Carolina's feminine adornment, her crown. She clenched her eyes for a moment before opening them again to her husband's reflection. She nodded. Ben expertly wrapped and tied the scarf around his wife's head.

"Beautiful," he breathed when he'd finished. Carolina's shaky smile presented him the best thanks she could.

Her emotions were so wild, volatile, she dared not speak. She had known losing her hair would be hard, but this drifted far beyond difficult. So much of her life—her identity even—had been tangled in the strands that covered her bathroom floor.

She examined her husband once more. The sadness remained on his face, but it was his love for her that radiated from him, warming her, strengthening her, encouraging her. Carolina rose into the arms of her husband to speak without words her emotions and love for him.

§

Carolina had never been able to choose one favorite season. Spring's brightness and new growth spoke to her gardener's heart, but autumn's spicy fragrance and promise of family traditions moved her heart's strings.

Those traditions included sports. During the World Series, Carolina found herself limited. Cheering with her typical enthusiasm was not a good option with her sore lips. Rachael found the solution, though. She brought her mom some pom-poms, and Carolina waved them enthusiastically during every game until the Braves' victory.

Since her third treatment was scheduled for the Tuesday after the team clinched their title, they drove down the day before to attend the team's victory parade. Carolina waved her pom-poms, while trying to remember to smile small. Rachael yelled loud enough for her and her mom. The red scarf caught the players' eyes. Several of them saluted Carolina from the top of the fire truck, and a team representative ran over with a signed World Series pennant. She nodded her thanks and blew them a kiss.

Carolina took her gift with her to the center the next day. Each time someone completed a treatment, she waved it while other patients cheered. The staff got in on the action, and someone brought in more pennants to hand out. Any opportunity to celebrate or smile found welcome on the chemo floor. That Halloween found an interesting mixture of baseball fever and costumes. Carolina observed the joy around her and offered thanks.

Thanks for the nurses, doctors and other caregivers who offered solicitude with kindness and love. Thanks for joy in simple activities like baseball games, parades and a day to dress up just for fun. Thanks for the gift of her husband and daughter and the love they shared.

The nurse removed Carolina's IV to a chorus of cheers, applause and waving pennants. Carolina's hand lightly covered her mouth as she fought off the giant smile fighting to get free. She thought again about the beauty in little things like smiles as she leaned back against the chair to listen to the nurse while they finished yet another treatment together.

§

Fall's Friday nights in the south find families snuggled beneath quilts on rock-hard bleachers cheering on their local high school football team. Carolina, Ben and Rachael cheered the Bellum Bears all the way to the state championships. By that point, the entire town knew the battle Carolina was fighting. The football players dedicated their state win to her in November.

The morning after the big game, Rachael snuggled with her mother in bed. Carolina felt the toll of the previous night's festivities combined with the past week's treatment. She smiled at the red head on her shoulder. Rachael's presence strengthened her, even on the roughest days. She rested her cheek on her daughter's silky crown and resolved to soak in every second like this she could.

"I'm proud of you, Mama." Rachael's tiny voice surprised Carolina. She lifted her head to look up at her mother. "I know you're fighting hard for Daddy and me, and I see how hard it is. I just want you to know I'm proud of you. And, I love you so much."

Matching tears formed in the corners of their eyes as Carolina whispered, "I love you so much, baby girl, and I'm so proud of you. You are such a kind, loving young lady. Oh, Rach! I'm excited for all you're growing up to be and to do. I know God's got amazing plans for you. You will be a remarkable woman of God, just as you are an incredible girl of God now."

She hugged her daughter close, watering her with tears and covering her with prayers for protection and peace through all her growing days to come. Carolina clung to the warmth of her daughter in her arms as she listened to each beat of her heart. She could still remember the tiny bundle Rachael made when the nurse handed her over, moments after birth. Though small, she had looked directly at her mother and gripped her proffered finger. She was strong as a newborn and even stronger as a preteen. Carolina knew her daughter would be okay. She could leave Rachael with confidence that she would continue to grow strong and sound. She pictured the beautiful woman she would become and reined in a sob at the thought of all she would miss.

Carolina's arms held Rachael tighter for all the heartbreaks she would miss comforting her through and for all the graduations, achievements and new jobs she'd never get to celebrate with her. She stroked her long hair as she thought of how she'd miss brushing it on her wedding day, and she held her daughter's hand as she envisioned it grasping a tiny one after powering through the grueling stages of labor.

She held her daughter's lifetime in her arms as she imparted every ounce of her mother's love to the little girl for whom she'd prayed.

Letters for Rachael

When You Fall in Love

If you're reading this letter, my precious girl, you believe you've met someone special enough to envision as the second half of your future. For me, a feeling told me I had met my forever. I was too young to know—or so many people said. They called it puppy love.

Why does the term puppy love come arm-in-arm with an eye roll? Do people really have that much trouble believing it can not just exist, but last? Love, in its purest form—unburdened by agendas and societal expectations, cracked hearts and wounded souls—is quite simple. Purest love is one heart opening to another and making a connection at their cores.

That happened to me in Mr. Atkin's chemistry class in tenth grade. My lab partner turned out to be the new guy—Ben Burns. He came from the land of movie stars and looked every inch the surfer with his toned physique, sun-kissed skin and eyes a deeper blue than the ocean in paradise. Of course, I had never been to the ocean, so my evaluation of his eyes was based on pictures. He turned out to be a baseball player instead of a surfer, too, but I still found myself drowning in the depths of those eyes—the ones he passed down to you.

He smiled that lop-sided grin of his, held out his hand and said, "Hey there! I'm Ben. Looks like you're stuck with me."

We were inseparable from that day on because, somehow, I just knew he was the one for me. It wasn't all that simple, of course. Life rarely is. What I couldn't know was how a horrible Beast would try to come between us and the future I believed in.

Thankfully, you haven't seen much of the devastating effects of drugs and alcohol. Long before you, though, drugs almost took your daddy. The spring after we met, his baseball team won the state championships. Our school had never been on top in any sport, so those guys celebrated for a few weekends in a row.

At one of the first parties, one of the guys brought in some LSD he'd gotten from his psychiatrist dad. Most of the guys took some—including Ben. That night began a battle he fought through our last two years in high school.

My parents wanted me to break up with him. My friends thought I was crazy. Even Ben looked at me on several occasions and asked why on earth I stuck by him. All I could say was I saw so much more in him. I saw all he could be, and I couldn't ignore how I had seen my future wrapped up with his when we first shook hands. They all thought I was wrong, and it's still something hard to explain. I simply chose to cling to that future and believe in it and in him. I have a feeling you may understand, though. I've seen that knowing in you, too.

Ben's use of the drug started small. He kept it to the occasional party. That's how it usually starts, I suspect. A little here; a little there. No big deal.

Until it is.

Toward the end of junior year, he started taking more. He liked that happy feeling and the deep thoughts he attributed to the acid. So, he figured more would increase the good. Instead, it led to some bad trips. He was seeing and hearing things that weren't there. I was rarely with him at those parties, but he started having flashbacks during the week. At the very end of our senior year, he still wasn't listening to my pleas for him to stop or get help. He didn't see how it was getting worse either. He still called himself a user, but I knew he was an addict. I'm still not sure why none of the adults at school tried to help him. My parents were too judgmental to stoop down and help anyone, I'm afraid. They just kept pushing me to dump him and stay far, far away.

You never met your grandparents—his parents—but they hadn't been much help either. His dad was an alcoholic, and his mom worked two hard jobs to keep them all fed and clothed. She didn't even realize he was in trouble until I caught up with her one day as she walked from her factory job to the gas station where she pulled a few night shifts each week.

I felt so bad telling her. The grayish bags under her eyes told me she carried an awfully heavy load already. When she understood her son had become a drug addict without her knowing, she just sat down on someone's front steps and cried soundlessly. Tears streamed down her face as she stared up at me, her eyes begging me to tell her I was wrong. To tell her that her baby boy was okay and wasn't held captive by a drug some people still thought could be good. It was anything but that. She talked to the school counselor, and we all talked to Ben. We let him know how much we loved him and wanted to help him. That's when he pulled away. He was so mad at me for telling his mom. He stormed away from me at school that day. It was a Friday. I remember trying to memorize his features through my tears because I worried it would be the last time I ever saw him. I had the worst feeling I'd ever had; I went home and prayed like I never had before. I didn't stop for supper. The next morning, I woke up beside my bed where my mom had found me, sound asleep with my hands still clasped. She'd draped a blanket over me, kissed my forehead and held the news she'd received until the morning.

Ben had used again that night. The paranoia hit him harder than ever before, and he thought he was being chased through our downtown by someone or *something that wanted to kill him. He was so convinced of the truth to this story that he launched himself through a glass window.*

You know that funny scar on Daddy's forehead that you always like to trace? Well, thankfully, that's the only scar he still has from that night. He broke his collar bone, some ribs and a wrist and had cuts from head to toe. He looked a mess when I finally got to see him later that day.

I was so scared to visit him in the hospital. I wasn't sure he'd ever want to see me again, but he apologized and promised he would never, ever walk away from me like that again. He also promised he'd start listening to me, so I told him he could prove that by going to church with me. I'm pretty sure he wasn't thrilled with my request, but he agreed.

It took a while, but once he called Jesus his Lord and Savior, our relationship switched from something feeble to something far stronger. He matured and began planning the future I'd always seen as possible for us.

Your father had others in his corner, too. Sheriff Marshall Winters was the gruff and crusty old guy who responded to the call the night Ben soared through the window. He decided Ben Burns would not slide back to drugs if he had anything to say about it. From that day on, he rode his backside—through rehab and summer school to get his high school diploma, to admission into Georgia Tech—in Sheriff Winters' hometown—and even to make it on the baseball team our sophomore year. He continued all the way through seminary. Together with Ben's mom, we loved him to and through every graduation.

He asked me to wait for him until he finished all his school. I didn't completely understand why we needed to wait to get married, and some of my friends warned me that he was going to break my heart. I knew he was my other half, though. When you know something that sure, time doesn't matter. I knew as sure as I knew he was meant for me that we would be together. A few years of waiting were simply fog over a lake, heavy for a moment but gone in the blink of an eye.

So, my sunflower, when you believe you've fallen in love, take your time. True love lasts and waits through absolutely anything. No storm or separation or Beast or tragedy can stop true love.

At the same time, you must know that while love may begin with a feeling, it's not a feeling. Love is a decision. And it's a decision you must continue to make day by day, moment by moment.

Love may choose you in the beginning, but you must choose it in the face of every trial and obstacle you both face. When you decide to give your love to someone, you're giving him the promise that you will continue to choose to love him through his good and bad and your mutual easy and anything-but-easy.

You won't be able to predict the challenges that await you. No one can. So, you have to be brutally honest with yourself. Is he worth walking through fire with? Is he worth walking through fire for? Answer those two questions candidly, and you will know if he is your forever.

IV

Planting Seeds

On Carolina's better days between treatments, she and Ben enjoyed "day dates"—picnics by the lake and coffee cup conversations, baking new recipes together at home and reading old favorite books. They would head to the park or the ice cream shop after picking Rachael up from school. On the worst days, Ben and Rachael took turns playing soft music and bathing Carolina's face and neck with a cool rag. Whatever the day brought, she insisted they spend as much time as possible together.

Two days before Thanksgiving, she endured the final treatment of her first round. Nausea and cramps set in strong, but she rested on the drive home and most of the day Wednesday. Despite her family's protests, Carolina insisted their holiday tradition continue. Anyone without family nearby had a standing invitation at the Baptist preacher's house each November. While the other women would do much of the cooking, Carolina had started Rachael's kitchen training over the past few weeks, and the budding chef was excited to try out her new skills.

The heat of the oven and warmth of the memories they made reddened the cheeks of the mother-daughter duo. They were both covered in flour from the homemade pie crusts Rachael had made. Carolina watched from the comfy chair Ben had brought into the kitchen as her daughter twirled around in celebration of her new skill. They spotted Ben standing in the doorway, smiling at them, and beckoned him to join them. When he began dancing with Rachael, Carolina felt her joy might overflow.

After the Thanksgiving dishes had been washed and the leftovers carefully packed away in anticipation of midnight cravings, the only remaining guests were Becky and her son, Jack. Ben challenged the kids to a card game battle while the women chatted in the living room.

Preachers' wives find the pedestals they're placed upon to be incredibly lonely; so, when a church member knocks down the pretentious column and extends a hand of friendship, it's welcomed. That's what Becky had offered Carolina soon after the Burns family had moved to Bellum. The women carried their children at the same time and gave birth a couple weeks apart. They raised those same children together, and Carolina had cried and prayed with Becky when her husband left without a goodbye. They supported one another as only two society outcasts can do. The preacher's wife and the lady whose drunk husband disappeared—the revered and the rejected.

"You look absolutely wrecked." Becky's worried expression became clear as they relaxed after the day's busyness. "Please let me bring you guys dinner—at least a few nights a week. I'd be happy to help out with laundry and cleaning, too."

"You always know exactly how to help. Right now, though, everything really is okay. Ben and Rachael are keeping this house cleaner than I ever did." The women embraced the simple normalcy of a shared laugh before Carolina continued. "As far as cooking goes—as long as I'm able, I want to cook every night with Rach. I want to pass down all the tips and tricks I learned the hard way, along with all of her and Ben's favorite recipes."

The women's smiles faded as they reflected on the reason for Carolina's urgency with her daughter's cooking education.

"I hate to leave her."

Carolina released sobs alongside her admission. She felt Becky cross to the arm of her chair and wrap her with friendship and love as their tears flowed like ice melting.

"I don't understand why this has to happen to you." Becky revealed her honest emotions.

Sobs eased to sniffs and shuddering sighs as the friends released their grief together. After resolved silence had settled over them, Carolina admitted, "I don't either. Sometimes I get so angry. Other times, I think that the grief over all I will miss might suffocate me. Then I'm reminded how infinitely better heaven will be. I do know that, and I rejoice in it; but I keep questioning how my task here on earth can be done when Rach is still so young and Ben is wrestling with what God's really called him to do—pastor a church or counsel addicts. I want to be here to support them both in all that's ahead of them."

The tears returned as Carolina added, "She's got so very much ahead of her."

Becky leaned her cheek on Carolina's head. "You have raised a strong, smart, precious little girl. That's a firm foundation you can be confident in. She's so good for my Jack. She puts him in his place, that's for sure." They laughed as they recalled every time Rachael had tilted her head and given her friend that look—the one that let him know he was being ridiculous or wandering out of line. She did it when he didn't quite see the need to share a toy or when he laughed when a bully called another kid a hurtful name or when he first got it in his head that curse words would make him cool.

"Every girl needs a mama. We should know; we didn't have them— not really. Rachael's going to need a mama, and you're a great one." Carolina looked up at her friend as she presented her plea. "Watch out for her? Please."

§

Ben stood in the vestibule of the First Baptist Church and cursed pine branches and twinkle lights. He could never tell church members how much he loathed the shedding wreaths and trees he spent his December cleaning up after and how his first task every day when he arrived at the church was to unplug the giant bulbs that flashed—why did they have to be the flashing kind? One of the husbands of the decorating ladies dutifully arrived early every morning to flip them all on. Ben would undo the man's work and head into his office, praying no one dropped by unexpectedly that morning and that he would remember to plug them back in before he left.

Saving electricity didn't seem to be a satisfactory reason to unplug Christmas lights. He'd tried that. The ladies who anticipated the first Sunday after Thanksgiving took their roles as holiday decorators seriously, and an unplugged strand or flipped off switch equated to an attack on their abilities to hang tinsel.

A preacher couldn't wander around bad-mouthing trees and garland at Christmastime anyway. People would hear that as "the crazy Baptist preacher hates Christmas." Rest assured, that tidbit would get passed around on rapid-fire whispers. Ben loved Christmas—well, he loved celebrating Jesus' birth. But, the greenery and fire hazard strands of lights and bickering over what color and size of bulbs are more "Christmas-y" felt out of place to him. Extraneous at best; gaudy at least; contrary to the Bible at worst.

Ben's sigh echoed in the empty room. He shook his head. More than ever he had no desire to be surrounded by colorful, flashing lights. Not when his wife was dying in front of his eyes.

He yanked cords from outlets … harder than necessary … before storming into his office and slamming the door. His seminary diploma clattered to the floor, and the tears he'd reined in for three months rushed from him like rapids surging down a mountain after a big spring thaw.

"Why, God? Why Carolina?" His anguish clung to each pleading word as he called out. Burying his face in his hands, Ben released his anger at watching the love of his life suffer. Sorrow at seeing the mother of his child in pain flowed from his heart. Frustration with the waiting and the torturous treatment she had to endure combined with confusion and uncertainty with what lay ahead of them. They had no way to know what the new scans she'd undergo the following week would reveal. The not knowing weighed heavily. Every emotion cut him deep with the jagged edges of their brokenness. He ached in his soul and felt this pain would completely undo him.

He had heard prayers like his many times—from others. He was the one to give answers … not the one to ask the *whys*. Of course, he knew the answers. God has a plan. Even though they can't understand that plan or all the *whys* and *hows*, they have the promise that they'll see one another again. One day, he would rejoin her in heaven where they'd live out eternity together with God. He knew her death would mean instant relief from the torment of the cancer growing in her body and from the treatments attacking both invaders and host. Those promises were, indeed, beautiful, wonderful, hopeful; but …

Ben wanted to finish out this life with his lover and best friend at his side. He wanted to dance with her at Rachael's wedding. He wanted to take her on a second honeymoon to see the Northern Lights she'd always longed to witness. He wanted to kiss her good morning and good night every day for the rest of his life. He wanted to spend long afternoons lost in her eyes, holding her tightly to his chest as their hearts beat in time together. He wanted to take the family trips they'd always talked about—the Grand Canyon; Washington, D.C.; Nova

Scotia; Boston for the Fourth of July; Seattle. He wanted the matching wheelchairs and the front porch rockers and the shouted *I love yous* when their ears stopped functioning but their love still beat strong. He wanted a full life together ... not a quarter of one.

He needed to grieve and rage and lash out. He squeezed his eyes around the emotion streaming from them. As he did, he pictured himself standing barefoot in darkness on an abandoned beach during a lightning storm. The crashing of the thunder, thrashing of the wild waves and slashing rain around him painted an outer picture of his inner emotions. As his tears gradually ceased, his emotions ebbed and his rage subsided, Ben whispered a prayer.

"Thank you, God, for allowing me to pray out my anger, to question your reasons, to cry out in pain. You are such a great, loving God that you not only heard and accepted my raging words and thoughts to you, but you listened and you comforted. I know this world is filled with sorrows and riddled with the cancer of sin. I know this is why such heartbreaking things happen—our bodies are imperfect; our world's imperfect. Nothing is as you created it to be. For this reason, we face death. But God, you don't make us face it in darkness. We have hope— the light of a hope of an eternity spent in your perfection. Guide my emotions. Clear my anger. Keep me focused on you and your promises and help me lead others through their grief and rage. Help me lead my family through this time. You've given me two incredibly strong ladies, but I know they will have moments where their strength fades, too. Help me lead them, guide them, love them. Let others look at our family and see you through the hope we have and the peace you've given us."

With Ben's amen, a smile surfaced. Whatever time they still had together was a gift he wouldn't miss. He packed a box with books and notepads, reignited the Christmas shine in the sanctuary, returned his diploma to its proper spot and carried his study home with him. He could write a sermon at home just as well as at the church—better, perhaps, without those obnoxious flashing lights.

8

Carolina was still asleep when he got home. She hadn't slept well the previous night. Exhaustion must have finally claimed her. She looked frail, draped on the sofa. As the sores in her mouth increased, her weight decreased. It was hard to eat when even a twitch of a lip can result in bleeding and pain. Ben's heart ached to see his wife's beautiful lips cracked and caked with scabs. He prayed the scans would show some improvement—some rainbow after the torrential storm she'd so bravely faced.

He quietly moved to their table and set up his makeshift office. They were sitting together on the sofa for meals these days anyway. Ben opened the Bible Carolina had given him when he told her he was going to seminary. Somehow, she had known his plans before he did. He smiled at the memory and then focused on the chapter in front of him: "O Lord, God of my salvation, I have cried out day and night before you."

Ben scanned down Psalm 88 to another verse: "Lord, why do you cast off my soul? Why do you hide your face from me?" Ben picked up his pen and wrote in his signature all-cap writing the title for Sunday's sermon:

GOD'S GREAT ENOUGH FOR ALL YOUR WHYS

By the time Carolina stirred, Ben had written his sermon.

"Hi there!" Her voice brought flutters to Ben's heart. He stood and crossed to where she leaned back against the wall across from him.

"How long have you been standing here?" Ben kissed his wife's forehead and led her back to sit at the table with him.

"Long enough to know you finished Sunday's sermon and feel okay about it." She squeezed his hand as her tone teased him. Over the years, she had joked that his face wore a thousand expressions when he wrote his sermons; so she could always tell what kind of message they were in for based on the evolution of the faces he made while working on it.

Ben shook his head at her but smiled his response. "Well, as usual, you are correct, my dear." He paused before continuing, "Actually, I just wrote out a sermon to myself."

"Oh! Those are always the best." Carolina winked as she smoothed back her husband's hair. It had grown longer than usual since she hadn't felt up to trimming it for him.

Ben brought her hand back into his as he caressed it with his thumb. "When I got to the church this morning, the blinking lights greeted me."

Her laugh interrupted him, and she speculated, "So, it's a sermon about anger?"

"As a matter of fact … yes. But, it's not just about the infernal lights." His expression sobered. "I've been angry at God for what you're going through, but I've been holding it in … until this morning. I let God have it. I asked all my whys out loud. I prayed out my anger at him for allowing this to happen. And, I told myself all the answers to the questions that I've given countless others over the years, but I finally learned something. God wants us to scream and cry out our anger as we ask those whys.

"This morning, I opened my Bible right up to Psalm 88, and it hit me that many of the Psalms are how God's children cried out to him. They contain all the raw emotion of people who are hurting and confused, sad and angry. God is such a great God that he willingly hears all our *whys,* and he's enough for them all. He hears us and then he calms us with his peace. That's why he gives us the other Psalms—the ones that praise all his works ... even the ones we don't understand. He wants us to lash out, but he doesn't want us to stay in that angry, hopeless state of mind. He is our hope even in the darkest moments."

Carolina smiled through the mist covering her emerald eyes. "God must have sent you that message for me today, too. I have been so angry, so hurt, so ... just plain mad. At God. At the doctors. At the world around me. Why did this have to happen to me? I've always eaten healthy, taken care of my body. How could I possibly be so filled with this crazy disease? Why do I have to die and leave you? Leave our baby girl?" The mist watered her cheeks as she lost her voice and accepted the shoulder her husband offered.

Together, they cried. Together, they prayed. Until, finally, together they rested in a peace and contentment—despite dark times—that only exists for those who trust God and rely on his goodness even in the face of uncertainty and trials.

Ben prepared a chocolate shake for Carolina. It was one of the few things she could ingest, thanks to the painful sores.

"Thank you." She smiled as traced the jagged scar on his forehead. "How I wish I could kiss you."

The sorrow veiling the twinkle of her eyes constricted his heart. "Well, I can kiss you." He folded her gently into his arms as he placed kisses on both cheeks, her nose, her forehead and both hands. "I love you more today than yesterday."

§

Carolina didn't get to sit in the front pew that Sunday to hear her husband preach the message God had sent their way. Instead, she and Rachael snuggled while watching a service on TV. The flu had hit little

Bellum in a big way. Whole families were going down at once, so Dr. Clarke informally quarantined his patient. With her immune system weakened, it would surely crumble if exposed to the rampant virus. Rachael's principal and teachers allowed her to do her schoolwork from home. Ben broke tradition and left the church without shaking everyone's hands.

Becky and Carolina kept up their daily chats on the phone instead of in person. They traded off the phones with their children who suffered withdrawals from not seeing each other every day.

Cancer attacks more than one person. It spreads beyond its host to prey on the emotions and mindset of every person who loves and cares for the one whose body's been ravaged.

That same community, however, becomes an undefeatable army when it bands together against a common enemy. Regardless of if the disease itself gets destroyed, that spirit of hopelessness and helplessness in its wake gets obliterated. Carolina's family, friends, community and cancer team had rallied around her and fought for her with prayers, cheerful messages and love.

Letters for Rachael

When You Say "Yes" to a First Date

Perhaps one day—many years from when I'm writing this—your father will fall asleep for a moment [or black out indefinitely], and you will get to say "yes" to a first date. I'm sure my advice would be far more specific if I were there with you, but I'll do the best I can from this distance. I've got three general tips for you.

1. Choose Wisely

You only get one "first" anything—date, kiss, chance to say "I love you." So, it's quite all right to be picky and choose wisely. The most important thing to look for in a potential boyfriend is if he believes in God and chooses to live for him. You'll be surrounded by many boys in Bellum who go to church with their families but may not be Christians. Watch how they act around their friends and away from parents and teachers. How they act when they're not worried about discipline tells a lot about their values. Notice how they treat their moms, sisters and girls in general—and how they talk about them. If a boy doesn't respect the women around him, he will not respect you. Stay far, far away from him. You deserve only the best—always remember that.

2. Move Slowly

Sure, "it's just a date" can be meant in a variety of ways, but remember this is "just a date." This isn't a lifelong commitment, but it's also not something to be taken lightly. You may one day marry this boy—if so, make sure this first date makes a great story to share with your kids. You may just as easily be best friends with his wife. So, don't do anything that would make that awkward. Or, you may never see him again, so don't give him something you can never get back. That brings me to my third piece of advice for you, my sunflower.

3. Guard Fiercely

You've probably heard many times by now to "guard your heart." But you may not know what that means or how to accomplish it—I certainly didn't when I was your age. Every time you open your heart—your emotions, your secrets, your innermost thoughts, your you-ness—to another person, you let down that guard. It can either be rewarded when a person returns your feelings or shared interests or mutual goals and results in a strengthened heart; or it will be damaged in some way by a person with the opposite intent.

Picture your heart like a giant field covered by pure white snow. It's beautiful and perfect and clean. Once you invite people into that field, though, some of that beauty will be altered. The marks they leave behind can be beautiful—precisely placed footprints passing by or magical snow angels. Or, those people can stomp through, dragging their boots as they trudge over the field, leaving ugly tracks or covering the glistening crystals with mud that leaves it a mucky mess.

You've experienced this in smaller ways when someone pretends to be your friend long enough to get something they want before turning their back on you or when a friend unintentionally says something that hurts you. These marks can be large, but they're often mild and simply aid in developing a better sense of discernment when it comes to reading people and building friendships. When you begin to open your heart to boys, though, you're throwing the gates open wider to deeper, more important areas of your heart. As a result, you're far more vulnerable from the start, and any damage done will result in larger and longer-lasting scars. If you've followed my first two tips, though, you should already have an advantage on this one. If you have carefully chosen a young man who loves God and you're proceeding slowly and cautiously, you could avoid any lasting, painful scars on your heart.

You need to guard his heart as well. While guys may hold their emotions closer than we do, remember that he is opening his heart to you as well—perhaps before you did, when he decided to take a chance and ask you out. If you know he's not right for you, don't lead him on. Consider his heart as you let him go gently. Sometimes I think guys' hearts are more easily cracked than ours because they do their best to hide their feelings. They don't want anyone—including themselves—to see their insecurities or needs. Don't let that fool you into flippantly playing with a young man's emotions. Their hearts are fragile, too—a snowy field you can beautify ... or destroy, causing him to build a higher fence around it for the next girl who comes along.

Here are a few extra tips for you about dating:

1. Don't dress how you think he wants you to dress. Dress the way you're comfortable, in a style you love. You may date more than one boy. Unless your daddy strikes it rich after I'm gone, you can't afford to change your wardrobe with each new boyfriend or date. This same principle applies to food, music, hobbies, movies and books. Guard yourself from making giant changes in your preferences, based on your date's opinions. Chances are, even when you meet "the one," you're not going to like all the same things. Your father eyes greasy cheeseburgers like they're manna from heaven; I see a heart attack on a plate and crave fresh veggies that make him gag. The thing is, I prepare his burgers the way he likes them and still enjoy my brussels sprouts as often as

I can. Neither of us compromised; we simply accepted each other's preferences.

2. Speaking of food—when a guy takes you out on a dinner date, don't order the lobster and filet mignon but don't order only a cup of soup either. Scan the menu and choose a few dishes in the middle price range that you would enjoy. Ask what he's considering ordering. His answer could be a good price point to go by as well. Also, consider that you may be too nervous to eat a lot. An appetizer and salad or dessert could be a good first date option. If you move to more dates, offer to pay for some of them or at least split the check. While he will most likely want to treat you, your offer will show him that you are willing to share the financial burden of dating and that you notice and appreciate his generosity.

3. Mind your manners. This seems silly for me to say because you already have such great manners. I'm reminded of a girl I went to junior high with. Her name was Peggy. Peggy liked to make people laugh, but she did that by burping, farting and blowing her nose—loudly. The boys all laughed at Peggy, right up until the seventh-grade spring dance. It turns out even junior high boys know that manners matter, and no one wants a date in a fancy gown who burps during dinner and farts on the dance floor. Of course, along those same lines, you may want to save the tacos and refried beans for at least date ten ... just in case. For your part, steer clear of a guy who has no manners. If you don't think he could behave at a nice restaurant or a play or may not be able to avoid embarrassing you on a group date, politely walk away, my dear.

4. Your appearance deserves your attention. I've already talked with you about makeup, so you know I believe less is more. When I talk about your appearance, I primarily mean that you have taken the time to be neatly put together and appropriately dressed in clean, wrinkle-free clothes. Show him you take care of yourself, and he will know you would do the same for him one day. When you make it clear that you respect and care for yourself, any young man who would like to continue to spend time with you will go out of his way to show you he respects and cares for you as well.

5. Ask questions. When you talk—and I certainly hope you do ... movies are fun, but not for two people trying to get to know each other—don't just yammer away about yourself and your friends and your favorite songs. Ask him questions—not yes or no questions—deep ones. Is he a dog or cat person and why? Is he close with his parents and in what ways? What does he want to do with his life? If he could visit anywhere in the world, where would it be and why? When you talk about yourself, don't ramble about the cool new song by your favorite singer or the pair of shoes your best friend has that you think are pretty. Open up and share some of your dreams and deep thoughts. Where would you like to be in five or ten years? What do you think about the latest school council topic or the candidates for an upcoming political election? If you can talk deeply now, perhaps you will be able to better communicate later should dating lead to more. If that's the case, clear communication is one of the greatest things any couple can have. If he freaks out at deep questions and future thinking, he's not ready for a relationship. Same goes for you ... if thinking ahead and considering a future that could include another person makes you sweat, perhaps you're not quite ready for a relationship beyond simple friendship either and need to set dating aside for a while.

6. Don't be nervous; be Rachael! Chances are, you'll do something stupid and embarrassing on a date. Everyone does. Drinks get spilled. Tongues twist funny, and the wrong word pops out. An unexpected joke leads to a spewed mouthful of soft drink—ask your dad about that one. And, your right foot suddenly turns left and down you go (not that I'd know anything about that). Laugh together and make the best of it. At the end of the day, he's just a guy and you're just a girl and you're both imperfect and you'll both mess up at some point. Accept each other's imperfections and help each other through them.

7. Have fun! I can confidently toss this one in the mix if you've heeded all my previous advice. Enjoy this time of getting to know another person. You may find you learn just as much about yourself in the process.

V

Watering Growth

Carolina's hands twisted in her lap as they drove to Atlanta a couple weeks before Christmas … and two days after her birthday. Dr. Kumari had the results of the scans she'd had done in Bellum the previous Friday. She was ready to know what the poison they'd been pumping into her had done—besides taking her hair and keeping her from eating without pain or kissing her loved ones.

By the time the doctor joined them in his office, Carolina had fluctuated between hope and despair so many times, she was already emotionally spent. His face, though, resurrected her hopefulness

"Your smile's making me happy, Dr. K. Do you have a good birthday/Christmas gift for me?" Carolina's teasing masked her worry.

"The news is positive." He smiled back at his patient. "Our torture seems to be hurting the bad guy, too. We cannot find any new growth in your scans, and a couple of the mets have, actually, shrunk—not much, but still going in the right direction. Plus, nothing has grown since your first scans."

The family cheered and celebrated and whooped and hollered. Nurses and other staff joined them, and Rachael danced enough for herself and her mother. Ben beamed at his wife.

"While you're still happy and pleased with me, let's get you ready for your next round of treatments. We're going to continue the same chemo as before, see if we can't hit this enemy while he's down." Dr. Kumari picked up a few charts and led them out of his office on his way to rounds.

"Do you want me to sit with you during your treatment today?" Ben asked.

Carolina gingerly dabbed at her lips, which had started to bleed from a smile that went too wide. She whispered, "I think I need a nap."

He kissed her forehead and whispered back, "I know you deserve it."

They left Carolina with her nurse—Ben to spread the good news to friends back home; Rachael to do schoolwork in the lobby. Carolina glanced back once at her daughter. The lights on the lobby's tree reflected all around her as she blew a kiss in her mother's direction. With it sailed a timid hope for a Christmas miracle.

§

New Year's Day 1996 opened the cover on a new calendar and began a new routine. Each night, Rachael drew a red heart for the days they spent together. Treatment days received an X instead—necessary, though not enjoyed.

Before she suggested the activity, Carolina had flipped to September and drew a thick red box around the third day. Every Tuesday after Labor Day, Carolina and Ben celebrated the day they met over beakers and behind safety goggles. If she could make it to September 3, they would be able to celebrate twenty-five years together, plus one more.

That was her purpose for the calendar. The nightly time with Rachael, whether they marked a heart or an X, became a welcome side benefit. She would braid or brush Rachael's hair while they chatted. Even on treatment days when Carolina was worn or when she had one of the headaches that had begun to plague her, she pulled from some hidden reserve mothers possess for the energy to spend quality time with her sunflower.

§

Ben stood in the doorway of his living room toward the end of February. Carolina and Rachael lay asleep together on the couch. From his position, they appeared so normal, so everyday; but Ben knew, when he got closer, he would see the tearstains on his daughter's cheeks and the evidence of another headache in his wife. Her shriveled body told the tale of a fighter who'd been a round and a half with chemo. He knew nothing about the scene before him was normal or everyday. He snapped a mental photo of the two people he loved more than anyone else on this earth and begged God—again—for a miracle to heal his wife, to transfer the invader from her body to his ... to let him take this torment away from her.

She had so much left to give and do, so much joy to share. And, Rachael needed her mother so much more than she needed him. As Carolina said, every girl needs her mama. He looked at the strand of her long red hair draped across her cheek and thought how like her mother she was, not just in looks but also in attributes. Mother and daughter were loving, loyal, funny, helpful. They were the sunshine in his days. His little girl had always been an old soul, but the past few months had matured her and reminded him how rapidly she would become a young woman. How could he ever raise a daughter without his wife's wisdom and empathy? He didn't want to do it, nor did he believe he could. She was the love of his life and his ideal helper for every aspect of their life together. He would be hopelessly lost without her. He needed Carolina. More, even, than his next intake of air.

Ben gasped and realized he'd been holding his breath. He shook his head. Now was not the time to think like this. A chance always remained—a possibility. God could choose to give them a miracle. These awful treatments could actually still be killing more than just his wife's body. Hope stood, and Ben chose to cling to that. As he shrugged off the remnants of his melancholy, he reminded himself of a truth he too often forgot—through all of life, even cancer, God was good. That was the greatest hope; the one he could trust. For now, as Carolina fought through the rest of this round, Ben chose to enjoy each moment together. He smiled as he thought about spending the evening ahead with his two best girls.

Carolina's eyelids fluttered until she focused her vision on the man in the doorway. She worked her dry lips into a semi-smile as she saw him looking back at her.

Ben mouthed, "Hello, beautiful."

The wider smile he earned pushed her lips a little too far, and she cringed. Before his worried expression, he held up a finger for her to wait. After some squinting on her part—blurry vision had recently joined her list of annoyances—she gave him a thumbs up. Ben knew she'd understood his message, so he walked down the hall for clean rags from the linen closet. When he returned, two shining freckled faces welcomed him.

"Hey, Chickadee!" Ben tousled his daughter's hair as he headed to his wife with a kiss for her nose, one cool rag for her lips and another for her forehead.

Carolina mimed a thank you, more with her tongue than anything else.

"Am I ready tonight, Mama?" Rachael asked excitedly.

Carolina's cheeks pressed up into a smile that twinkled in her emerald eyes, and Rachael whooped her way to the kitchen.

"Our little birdie's flying solo on dinner tonight?" Ben asked. He received his answer in the form of a few escaped tears. Noting the mixture of pride, joy and sorrow behind them, Ben kissed them away before a clatter drew him to the kitchen to check on their budding executive chef.

"Everything okay?" Ben recognized the worry lining her face.

"Yeah, it is, Daddy. Really. I just …." Rachael bit her lower lip and glanced at the lids scattered at her feet before continuing. "I just want to do it perfect so Mama doesn't worry."

Ben crossed the tile floor to wrap Rachael in his arms. "No one does anything perfectly, especially not their first time. But you don't need to worry. Your mama in there is proud as she can possibly be already. If you make her any prouder, her head may pop."

Rachael's giggle caused a hitch in Ben's breathing as he was reminded—yet again—how she was still a young girl, accepting more responsibility than some adults. Ben tilted his daughter's chin up toward him. "Do you need a sous chef?"

She smiled and shook her head. "I got this … I think." Her wink let him know she'd overcome her nerves, and she shooed him away. "Go check on Mama and see if she's up for a movie tonight."

Ben saluted as he headed back to find his wife sitting up and looking somewhat rested, a rarity those days.

"You look ready to run a marathon." Ben chuckled when his wife rolled her eyes at him. "Rach wondered if you're up for a movie tonight."

Carolina's face answered clearly. She loved to do anything with her family; and, even before cancer upended their lives, movie nights had always been a favorite. She whispered, "Let Rach pick."

"You got it!"

After a dinner of pork chops, mashed potatoes and black-eyed peas that Rachael planned—with her mother's limited eating ability in mind—and prepared start to finish, the family snuggled up to watch her favorite, *The Little Mermaid*. Ben looked from his wife to their daughter and felt a fullness of love in his heart.

Letters for Rachael

When You're Ready to Say "I Do"

My beautiful sunflower, my eyes are misty as I write this letter because I'm picturing you as you will be when you're ready to read it. Gone are the pigtails and bright, wide-eyed curiosity of the girl I've watched grow and know so well. In her place, the beautiful woman of God I would have loved to know.

I am so proud of you and happy for you as you prepare to glide down the aisle to the man you join for your future. If you are reading this, you should have already read my advice for you on your first date and for when you thought you met "the one." If you read those and took them seriously, then I have no warnings for you.

If, however, you're filled with panic-inducing doubt, and he and your joint future are not the overflowing, joy-filled thoughts on your mind, walk away now. Don't wait to finish reading; just set this aside and call it off.

Now that that's past and you are positive and excited to begin the rest of your life with this man of your dreams, then Congratulations! He is a lucky man, and I am so happy for you both. I prayed for him before you were even born. Did I ever tell you that? I did. Even back when I was a teenager, I prayed for my future husband, our future children ... and their future spouses. It's a shame I don't know the lucky guy's name. I wonder *if that's something God will fill me in on when I get to heaven. Hmmmm ...*

Anyway, I do have a few thoughts to share with you about marriage. It's not all flowers and candy and romance and dates and fun.

No ma'am.

Marriage is broken dishwashers, flat tires, dying air conditioners, empty bank accounts and sick kids—all at the same time. It's bills and worry and stress. It's juggling family and responsibilities and time. It's disagreeing over how to roll the toothpaste and fold the towels. It's the absolute terror of realizing newborns don't come with care manuals. It's bearing one another's burdens all the time for the rest of your lives.

Marriage is also a daily deciding to put the other one first, to love despite the disagreements, to keep marching through whatever rocky terrain, mountains or valleys you encounter—together. And it's a daily deciding to do all this through Christ. If he's not the center of your marriage, you're trudging uphill through a mudslide while carrying a 500-pound anvil with a frayed rope.

Marriage is also flowers and candy and romance and dates and fun. It's laughter and tears—together. It's making a family together, and it's being with your best friend every day for the rest of your life. It's waking up to your lover's face every morning and kissing him every night. It's doing life with your beloved and knowing you have found the one to whom your heart belongs and for whom it beats true. Marriage is a melodious duet gifted to us from the Creator of love. It is an imperfect image of Christ and his church.

With that in mind, Rachael, I point you to Ephesians. You should read chapter 5. You probably already know it by heart, but have you ever really thought through what it means? In my younger days, many women hated this chapter and took up arms against the concept of "submit to your own husbands," but they missed the beauty of those words because they didn't read the whole chapter—not carefully or thoughtfully anyway.

See, that second part goes to husbands; and both halves are required to make a whole marriage. The godly husband and wife should mirror Christ and his church. To be loved like that ... wow!

In my prayers for your future husband, I asked God to bring you a man who loves him most of all so he can love you like Jesus loved us. As he loves you, I pray that he grows every day closer to God so that he can lead you and lead your children in God's word. I pray he will love you and care for you as he cares for himself. I pray he looks out for your very best interest in every decision he makes. He's got a high calling in caring for you and loving you this way.

And so, my dear, I urge you to learn how to submit to this man God has prepared for you. Submit to him in love as you support him, encourage him, pray for him, challenge him and walk beside him in this life you're beginning together. Talk with him, discuss with him, pray with him. Read and study the Bible with him. Learn together, grow together, serve together.

Marriage requires a heap of hard work—every single day. You can't be lazy about your relationship and expect it to be a good one. You can't go your separate ways and do your own things and expect to be close. Spend time together. Do fun things together. Do hard things together. Do things he likes. Do things you like. Do things you both like. Do new things together. And, when the kids come, don't stop setting aside time to do things together—just the two of you.

Your kids are important—super important—but remember, you only have them for a few short years. You'll have your husband with you for the rest of your lives. You will both change a lot as you're raising your children. If you don't intentionally spend time together during those years, communicating and sharing your changes and your struggles, you may not recognize the person you're sharing a house with when your children drive away to college.

As you prepare for your big day, don't let your vows get lost beneath the flowers, food, decorations and favors. Remember that you are making a promise to one another—for life.

When you choose your dress, shoes and hairstyle, choose comfort. It will be a long day full of pictures and waiting and family and friends. Above all—be comfortable. Here's a tip: if you're wearing a long dress, chances are no one will see if you're barefoot or in slippers instead of pinchy heels anyway. When your father and I got married, I wore a big frilly dress. I also chose the huge heels. I regretted that.

Years later, we barely remembered anything about that day. It's okay to keep it simple, if that's what you want; it's also okay to have a huge wedding if that suits you both better. Choose what's right for you two and don't let other people dictate how you dedicate yourselves to one another.

One thing I would encourage you to do—have a special time planned for the two of you to meet together alone, preferably before the ceremony. (That whole bad-luck-to-see-the-bride-before thing is highly overrated.) Give yourselves a moment to connect, to remember in the midst of all the hustle and bustle and crowd of people what you're there for and who your day is all about. It's about you and your husband joining your lives together with God at the core.

Your father and I decided to have all our pictures made before the ceremony so we would be done afterward. Before we took any photos together, though, we asked to have the sanctuary to ourselves. I walked down the aisle to him as we saw each other for the first time in dress and tux. We prayed together; we talked together; we laughed together; and we took that time to relax and remember why we were there. It was perfect and exactly what I needed.

Aside from keeping God in the center of your marriage, the next most important thing for a strong marriage is communication. If you don't talk—deeply, honestly and candidly—every day, everything else will be a hundred times harder. If you want a unified marriage, talk. If you want an amazing love life—yes, I said it ... God created it, enjoy it!—communicate. If you want to remain best friends, ask questions and share. If you want to grow closer every day and avoid feeling like roommates, converse.

I think that's all the advice, wisdom and encouragement I can give to you, my precious daughter, as you prepare to be a bride. I do wish I could be with you. I always dreamed of this day for you. In my dream, though, I was there to help you with your hair and makeup and dress. I was there to hand you your "something old, something new, something borrowed and something blue." I was there to calm your nerves, share your joy and witness your beautiful walk of love. I am there with you, though, my Rachael ... in your heart. My love will always be yours. I love and miss you so much. Enjoy your special day. I hope your love and marriage are as beautiful and wonderful as mine with your father.

VI

Pruning Weeds

Early in March, Ben loaded their suitcases for another trek to Atlanta, his hope still bolstered by the encouragement they'd received in December. They had requested to hear her results on Monday. They planned to celebrate with a special dinner before her next round of Tuesday treatments. With Carolina's mouth nearly healed and her appetite picking up, Ben wanted to make the most of the relief. The moment Dr. Kumari walked into his office, however, the sunlight streaming through the window was snuffed out quicker than a candle's flame in a hurricane.

"I am so sorry. It has spread ... to your brain."

Ben and Carolina held hands as they looked across the desk at the oncologist who interlaced his fingers before resting his chin on them. Ben saw the weight pressing on the doctor. He considered what a trying profession this man had chosen and prayed for his strength and encouragement.

Ben evaluated his wife. Physically, she was far different from when they first sat in those chairs nearly six months previously. Her bloodshot eyes stood out even more with the dark circles beneath them. The toll the treatments took marked Carolina's body and spirit. He read the exhaustion in her slumped shoulders and searched for a glimmer of hope in her stoic expression. He rubbed her hand with his thumb as Dr. Kumari spoke.

"This is not the news I had hoped we would get. We do have options, though. Your odds haven't gotten any better, of course, but there is always a chance. I know you are worn and short on hope, but I do have a treatment plan I'd like you to consider."

Carolina shifted slowly in her seat as she tightened her grip on Ben's hand and rubbed the edge of her blouse.

"This would be an aggressive plan. We would specifically target the new met and the other largest ones with radiation while simultaneously using a new chemo."

At Carolina's gasp, Ben put his arm around her shoulders.

Dr. Kumari's voice quieted as he continued. "This would be an all-eggs-in-one-basket approach."

Carolina's voice rose soft but strong. "So, this would be an all-out attack. A last stand?"

His slight nod confirmed her evaluation. "I'll put in the orders for the treatment to begin tomorrow, but you guys take tonight to talk it over. When you get here in the morning, you can let me know your decision. We'll be prepared, whatever you decide."

That night held no celebration. Instead, the family held one other. Tears flowed as they prayed for strength and peace. Exhausted, Rachael fell asleep against her mother's chest at the same time Carolina sank into the depths of much-needed rest. Ben held his girls and watched them both breathe. Up, down. In, out. The oxygen flooded into them, filling their bodies with life for another moment. He felt the carbon dioxide escaping to make room for what they needed. He envisioned the path the air took inside his wife's body. Did it leap over the tumors, did it avoid them all together or did it simply blast around them? Did it discover even more growth of the monstrous disease than the scans showed?

How did it get there to begin with? Why? *Why, God, why?*

Ben pulled his wife to his chest as he closed his eyes and let her living breaths lull him into a deep sleep.

Late that night, Carolina stirred, drawing Ben from the slumber that had claimed him. He looked down at his wife. She was gazing at Rachael, still sleeping soundly in her arms. She bent to kiss her daughter's silky hair, leaving a damp trail behind when she looked up at Ben.

"I had hoped ...." She left her sentence unfinished.

He nodded. "Me too."

"Ben?" He knew what she was thinking before she spoke but nodded anyway. "I'm not sure how much longer I can fight."

He moved gently to avoid waking Rachael and turned to face his wife. "I am here for you, and I support you however you choose to fight ... or not fight ... this." He choked on his next words. "I only wish I could take this from you ... or fight it for you. I wish it were me instead. Seeing you in this much pain tears my heart to pieces."

Their emotions continued to flow as they held one another. Finally, Carolina said, "Thank you for loving me, for encouraging me. I never could have faced this as I have without you. I am so thankful God gave me you."

Cheeks together, the couple bent over their sleeping child as they prayed for wisdom.

Back in the doctor's office the next morning, Carolina looked to Ben, cleared her throat and declared, "Let's make it a good fight. I'm ready to make one final stand."

Ben didn't need to ask the question lingering on his lips. He knew she was certain. His heart broke as he thought of the suffering ahead for his bride, but he dared to hope—one last time—for a miracle.

§

Rachael settled in for a day of caring for her mother while her father was away at a meeting. Over the past month, she had watched her mother endure two treatments with the new chemotherapy and ten days of radiation. It was a month-long onslaught that left her mother branded as a warrior in the gallant fight against cancer.

The bright side to the new poison Carolina was receiving centered on relief from some of the previous side effects. She could finally eat without pain, which meant she didn't look so much like an unstuffed scarecrow. The new torture brought its own list of issues—joint pain and tingling in her hands and feet. Those, combined with headaches and dizziness, made walking without help nearly impossible. Rachael and her dad would hold Carolina up when she was too weak to lean over a basin and vomit. They cried as they watched her grow weaker from this final vicious treatment.

Rachael breathed a prayer of thanks that the radiation was over as she re-tied her mother's scarf over the burns on her head. She fought tears as she considered all her mom had endured in the hope that their family could have a little more time together.

Through all the pain and exhaustion, her mother never ceased to smile. She frequently whispered, "I love you," to her husband and daughter. Each day she inched one foot forward as far as she could, even when a treatment would push her five steps back. She watched the calendar and cheered as energetically as she was able each time Rachael Xed off another treatment day. One down, one less to go.

Rachael patiently held straws at the best angle for her mother to receive water or scooped another cup of ice chips. She stroked her hand when she slept and instituted weekly mani-pedi days. She read out loud to keep her mom from getting bored. Since Carolina's diagnosis, they had read the *Anne of Green Gables* books and *Black Beauty* and they were starting *Jane Eyre*. It wasn't the easiest book for an eleven-year-old, but Rachael read and loved it anyway. It was her mother's favorite, so she was determined to read the entire book for the woman who'd taught her to read.

After reading one chapter that afternoon, she lay with her head against her mother's thigh, clasping her slender hand in both of hers. Next week would be Rachael's twelfth birthday, but she had no desire to celebrate. Her silent tears slid unchecked onto the bed as she watched her mother's face, nearly peaceful and pain-free as she slept. She knew the reality of her mother's diagnosis. As her eyes followed the scars— seen and unseen—across her mother's body, Rachael also knew she didn't want to watch her suffer any more. She didn't want to lose her mother—the woman who had prayed for her, carried her, changed her, rocked her, taught her, raised her, fed her, clothed her and loved her. But she also didn't want her to live in such agony. Rachael squeezed her eyes as she asked God to grant a miracle ... or give her mother a break. She softly kissed her mother's hand and rested with her.

Letters for Rachael

When You Question Your Worth
& Wonder How to be a Friend

I decided to link these two together, which may seem odd. I don't have a clear picture of when you will be reading this, but I'm guessing it will be soon—junior high or early high school. The reason I combined these two is, our worth often becomes entwined with the friendships we have. More often than not, that's a horrible setup.

First off, my darling daughter, remember you are a daughter of the King of kings. You are God's child, a princess. Above any other title you will ever earn or take on, this is the core of who you are and it—not any other title or any person—determines your worth. You understood on the bright June morning when you gave your life to Jesus that he died for you. He purchased your freedom and paid the debt of your sins. You were bought by him for an eternity with him; so you, my sunflower, have eternal worth—royal worth.

I cannot make you understand or believe that. I cannot make you remember that. I can only give you these words and pray that God directs them into your heart and brings them back to your mind when you are questioning your worth in this world—because you will.

It seems that life tends to be harder on women these days. We're constantly hit with ads that tell us we're not pretty enough or sexy enough or accomplished enough or smart enough or—simply—enough.

That's a lie that Satan will toss in your face again and again and again. The truth is you are enough. You are enough for whatever God has planned for your life. You are enough for the people he has placed in your life, too.

And that brings me to my second topic—friends. Your friends—your true friends—will see your worth and know you are enough as well. If anyone asks you to change for them or says you're not enough, they are not true friends and not worthy of your time, energy or deepest love.

So, for those, back away. Don't apologize. Don't justify sticking around. Just get away. It's as simple— and difficult, too, I know—as that.

For those who are true friends, cling to them, love them, be there for them. Friendship is another beautiful gift from God. Treat it as such and treat them as the worthy, enough people they are. Be a good friend. Be there for them. At some point, a friend will go through a rough time. Just be there. Often, that's all you need to do.

Communication strengthens all relationships. Talk to each other. Share your hopes and dreams. Share your fears and uncertainties. Encourage and uplift each other on the down days and cheer with each other on the great ones.

Watch out for misunderstandings. Those are the enemies to friendships. A shrug or sigh taken the wrong way can lead to hurt feelings. A word can cut deeper than a knife. Talk. Communicate. If you are hurt, tell them. Make sure they do the same. Open, candid conversations mend misunderstandings before they widen to something far worse.

Protect your friends. Stand up for them when others mistreat them or spread lies about them. Protect them from wrong relationships and from themselves. Make a pact to be honest with one another, no matter what. If they are doing something that will lead to their harm or if they are allowing someone into their life who is not good for them, you have to tell them—even when they don't want to hear it. And then be there for them when they finally agree with you—even if that takes a long, long time.

Be kind to all as you always have been, Rachael, but choose your friends wisely. Find those true friends who recognize your worth and commit yourself to be and do the same for them.

VII

Nurturing Soil

Rachael's twelfth birthday arrived, despite her desire to not celebrate. She woke to French toast in bed and a day off school. She spent the whole day with her parents, talking, playing games, taking a picnic lunch by the lake and watching movies afterward while her mom rested. Carolina had a good day since radiation was over and she'd had almost a week since her last treatment; however, she could only go so long before fatigue claimed her.

Becky and Jack joined them for supper and the cake Rachael had insisted she make from scratch. Carolina gave instructions from her kitchen director's chair, as they'd started calling it. They were each coated in batter and icing by the time they were done baking, and Ben clutched his sides as he tried to stop laughing at them.

Rachael sank into her bed that night. She noticed how worn her mother's eyes looked as Carolina tucked her in with a kiss—a sign of affection she hadn't realized how much she had missed. "Thank you for making today so special. I didn't really want to celebrate. You've been so exhausted ... in so much pain. You didn't have to do all this."

Her mother's smile bore traces of her sorrow as she said. "Yes, I did. Because this day? I have been looking forward to this day for way more than twelve years."

Rachael giggled at her mom's exaggeration. They both grew serious again as Carolina continued. "Celebrating with you, doing fun things like we did today ... these are the little things that make me feel better. They're what I've been fighting for. I hope this was at least half as happy a day for you as it was for me."

"Nope—more than twice as happy." Hands clasped, they smiled as they reveled in the remnants of their uplifting day.

Carolina whispered, "I have one more surprise. Close your eyes and hold out your hands." Rachael giggled as she obeyed. She felt something solid, yet soft and arched an eyebrow, impatient to peek. At Carolina's song of, "Open your eyes!" Rachael discovered a pink velvet heart-shaped box resting in her palms.

"Is this your ring? Your real emerald and diamond ring that grandma gave you when you turned thirteen?" She opened the lid to answer her own question before looking back at her mother's face. "But ..."

"I know. I had told you we'd carry on the thirteenth birthday tradition, but I wanted to move it up. I think you're responsible enough for such a special piece of jewelry." Carolina nodded as Rachael sought permission to slip on the glittery ring. "Perfect fit. The biggest reason to give it to you now is to witness that joy on your face and to see you wear it. I love you, my beautiful birthday girl."

Carolina kissed her daughter's forehead and wished her one more happy birthday. Rachael clutched the ring as she held her mother's hug a few seconds longer than usual.

"Thank you, Mama. I love you."

§

Carolina enjoyed her most energetic days the week after Rachael's birthday. As she walked onto her deck that Thursday morning, a slight chill stubbornly clung to the morning air. She couldn't remain inside another minute, though. She longed to sink her hands into the soil and feel its life-giving power.

She sighed at each sign of neglect her eyes lit upon. They were details no one else would notice, but she did. She knew her garden intimately, and it knew her.

Her roses spoke to her. Ben laughed when she said that. She told him how plants were like children; they just required more careful attention to hear what was needed. That morning, the roses' message drifted to her on the breeze along with their unique mixture of sweet fragrances. They had missed her spring pruning and mulching. But, roses were forgiving. They continued to whisper in rustles and shuffles that called to mind phrases of Psalms and favorite hymns, poems by Wordsworth and Shakespeare. She had always said roses were literary. Ben laughed at that, too.

A cloud drifted toward the west, unveiling the sun and allowing its rays to reach Carolina's drawn face. She raised it, eyes closed, as her wan skin drank in the heat. A smile danced across her lips as she recalled countless springs in this Eden she had carefully nurtured—from the spring morning her water broke beside the Mexican Bush Sage, to Rachael's first steps between vegetable rows, to the blistering summer day last year when she first felt something sinister growing inside her body as she watered her herbs.

Carolina beamed beneath the warmth of the sun and her harvest of memories. Opened again, her eyes landed on the rose bush in the center mound of her garden—her 'L.D. Braithwaite'—the one she'd dreamed into existence. Back in Idaho, she had planned a garden of her own. It began the day she surrendered her sorrows over not being able to have a child. Something about the nature that surrounded her that day spoke to her. Before she began to build this garden nearly thirteen years ago, she imagined a perfect crimson rose—bright and beautiful with perfectly round blossoms. Years later, Carolina visited a rose grower who'd received some special roses bred in England. As she perused the plants, her eyes landed on her dream rose. It became her garden's centerpiece, and she added more roses over the years, all from David Austin Roses, to complement and highlight her favorite.

She smiled as she recalled each one she'd chosen over the years. Everything in her garden was as she had originally dreamed it. Her vegetable rows at the back of their property against the pine trees produced great crops with each season. Over the past two summers, she and Ben had sweated together laying flagstone pavers for a path Carolina had envisioned for years. The path wound around each of her ten round flower beds. Its widest portion circled the eleventh—and center—bed that housed her special rose, surrounded by a ring of smaller purple-crimson roses. For Carolina's birthday, Ben had hired some guys from the nearby mission to help him build a low stone bench around that bed. She loved to sit there and watch the busyness of the bees and butterflies that made themselves at home in her garden.

As the memories warmed her, Carolina walked across her deck and down the stairs, lifting her trowel on the way. She kneeled by her herb bed that lined the deck. Eyes closed, she inhaled deeply. Rosemary, thyme and sage teased her nose. A breeze wafted hints of peppermint, chocolate mint and spearmint from the hanging baskets around the deck and along the back of their house. She wiggled her hands deeper in the cool earth and delighted in the sensation of the dirt trickling through her bare hands. She'd never liked garden gloves. The coolness of the nurturing soil she entrusted to grow her plants invigorated her.

As she felt its softness, she looked across the rose beds to the empty space on the west side of their house. As she gazed at the land's potential, a vivid image appeared in her mind. She began to count days in her mind. How long they would take to grow. How long they could last. Five rows should do it. She smiled as she opened her eyes again. The flowers she would plant would be a surprise to cheer Ben and Rachael after she was gone and remind them she wasn't separated from them forever; she was waiting for them.

"Well, aren't you prettier than these magic flowers you grow?" The amused voice paused the vision of the future in Carolina's mind and widened her smile.

"Do you have a morning off?"

Becky descended the deck's steps to her friend. "I sure do, and I can't imagine anywhere else I'd rather spend it. I hated to interrupt your daydreams. I haven't seen you this happy and peaceful in far too long."

"Earth, air, fire and water." Carolina patted the ground, gestured in the wind to the sun above and then pulled up a handful of damp earth. "The elements bolster the spirit, strengthen the body and sharpen the mind."

Becky's laughter rolled across the yard as she teased, "You sound like a textbook or one of those New Age, self-help books."

"In that case, I won't repeat it for Ben—or mention it to the ladies at Bible study." Carolina joined in her friend's humor. "I was just planning a new flower project. It's a surprise for Ben and Rachael, but I might need some help from you and Jack to pull it off. Think you guys could give me some help mid-July to early August?"

"That sounds an awful lot like hard work ... but, of course!" Becky's eyes sobered as she memorized her friend's face. "I'm so thankful you've found peace and contentment as you live this precious time, but I'm not finding the peace, Carolina. You're my best—my only—friend in this town." She swiped a rogue tear with her thumb and quickly added, "I'm not going to ruin today's beauty with my sappy complaints, but I'm struggling with this contentment thing. Let me know when you've got some words of wisdom on that one, Mrs. Rev."

The women chuckled at her pet name. Carolina had confided to Becky long ago how hard it was to be the pastor's wife and how sometimes she wished Ben had been a carpenter or banker or anything where the wife wasn't expected to help with everything and act a certain way for everyone. Becky had never thought of her friend as "the preacher's wife" or expected her to say or not say certain things or dress a certain way. She was simply her friend with whom she loved spending time.

Carolina picked up her trowel and pressed it handle-deep in the soil beside her. "I do know this is so much harder on everyone else at this point. I wish it weren't that way, but—like I told Ben—I'm going to do my best to leave you all with the most beautiful memories I can. And, if heaven has rocky road ice cream and waffle cones, you can be sure I'll be waiting there when you arrive with two for us to share." She nudged Becky and winked. They'd always found humor, even in deep conversations.

"Since you're so full of heavenly wisdom and we're all focused on living and such …" Becky took her turn to wink. "I'm worried about Jack and whether or not I'm a good enough mom. My mind keeps me worried that he'll follow in his dad's footsteps—that he'll lose himself in a bottle one day and run away to try to find himself. And, the worst part is, my biggest reason for the worry is totally selfish … I don't want to be alone."

Carolina rested a hand on her friend's knee as sobs shook her shoulders and tears sprinkled the basil and oregano. As Becky sighed and cast off the rest of the moisture, Carolina rose and offered her hand to Becky. They walked, arms linked, to the deck where they sank into a couple of cushioned chairs.

Once they'd gotten comfortable, Carolina turned to her friend. "First of all, you are exactly enough. I know that because God chose you to mama Jack. God gave you the exact mother heart you need for that precious, precocious, mischievous, bundle-of-energy boy of yours."

Becky whisked away a couple more teardrops as she laughed and nodded. "That's Jack, in a nutshell."

Carolina continued. "Let's just say—worst case scenario—Jack does follow in his dad's footsteps. Will you love him any less?"

Becky shook her head, her eyebrows knit together.

"Exactly. You will be right here, loving him and praying for him. But, we don't have to dwell on that. Instead of fretting about all the what ifs, camp out in the right nows. I know you wish you had better work hours and could spend more time with him, but think through the time you do have. How can you maximize every minute of it?"

"Well, I could do more things he enjoys with him. He's growing up so fast; I'm not entirely sure what those things are anymore."

"Then, there's your first step—talk to him. As far as your last part goes, no one wants to be alone. We were created for company. Why do you think you fixate on ending up alone?"

"I guess because I felt so abandoned when Jack Sr. left. I was just a baby when I married him and he brought me across the country to this tiny town. Not that I left anyone behind, but I didn't exactly get the red-carpet treatment when we got here. I think everyone but me saw right away what kind of guy he was. Anyway, I didn't have anyone but him until you moved to town and invited me to church. Until then, I had felt so completely alone. Even on the few nights he wasn't out drinking, I was still all alone beside him on the couch. When he left, I had no idea what I was going to do—a single mom, no family, no skills. I was terrified."

"But you survived. You found a way to provide for you two, and you have been a wonderful mom. Truly. You have found ways to be both mom and dad for him. You can handle anything with God. I firmly believe that. And, one day, you will get to chase your dreams, so you better start figuring out what those are."

"Last time, I had you." Becky's smile vanished quicker than it appeared. She shook her head. "I don't know. I'm just having a ridiculous pity party over something that may or may not ever happen. The truth is, I was young and foolish when I said 'I do' and had never figured out—or even thought about—a dream to work toward. Once he came into my life, I decided he was my dream and never considered needing another."

"It's not too late for dreams now, you know. What are some ideas you have?"

"I don't think Bellum's a place for dreams to come true." Becky smiled at her friend's prodding. "The only thing I ever considered for more than a few minutes was opening a bookstore. You know, the kind with special story times for kids. I don't see that being too popular here."

"So, move!" Carolina's laugh echoed throughout her garden. "You keep tossing over excuses, I'll keep hitting them out of the park."

"You sound like Ben with your baseball talk," Becky teased. "But, you're right. Maybe. One day."

"God's not going to plant a strong desire in your heart that keeps growing without giving you the ability to achieve it."

"You know, you can be annoying when you're right all the time." Becky rolled her eyes.

"Maybe. But, you still love me." Carolina's expression darkened. "Switch?"

"Please."

During their early days of motherhood, Becky and Carolina began taking turns sharing their frustrations and concerns. Whenever one had released her pent-up frustrations, the other would request "Switch?" to take her turn.

Carolina took a deep breath. "The one thing I cannot stop worrying about is my sweet Rach growing up way too fast through all this. She's always been an old soul, and I can see her taking on way more responsibility and worry than any twelve-year-old should. I don't want her to bury her grief without processing it because she feels like she's responsible for taking care of Ben or putting on a brave face or something like that. I worry she'll keep her sorrows hidden."

Becky took her friend's hand. "Rachael is the most mature child I have ever met, no doubt. And, I completely understand your worry. You need to talk to her about it, though. You've been open and honest with her about everything that's happened. That was the best call, by the way; especially with how intuitive she is. Anyway, tell her your concerns. Talk to her about how to process grief. She may be wanting to ask you this same thing but may not be sure how. While you're at it, you better prepare that husband of yours for how to handle the emotional rollercoaster that is a teenage girl."

"You're right about that." Carolina took both of Becky's hands in hers. "I do have one request for you, though. I know we've already talked about this, but please check in on her every now and then? Be a shoulder to lean on and a listening ear for the times when a dad's not who she needs?"

Becky ignored the moisture welling in the corner of her eyes as she squeezed her friend's hand. "You and I carried our babies together and raised them alongside one another. You're about the only one I can't beat at loving her. Of course Rachael can call me—anytime."

As the spring winds swept away their spoken cares, the women moved indoors for a more carefree chat over coffee.

§

The rest of April passed with another treatment and continued weekly blood tests. Carolina's headaches became more frequent, and the doctors prescribed pain medicine to help with them and with the searing pains in her arms and legs. On her better days, she spent as much time as possible in her garden. She did some of the pruning she had missed earlier in the season. Ben often joined her, and she began to teach him the art of pruning, mulching and watering. By her final chemo treatment on May 7, she had him talking to her flowers.

A couple weeks later, she had her final scans. When they sat down in the doctor's office at the end of May, Carolina didn't expect a positive result. Dr. Kumari entered and sat on the desk directly in front of them. Carolina knew then this would not be the news they'd all longed to hear.

"Ben, Carolina, I am so sorry. The treatments have not done what we had hoped. All your mets are the same as before, but the one on your brain has grown and spread. We discovered new spots on your bones as well. There are different types of radiation and chemo we can try, if you would like."

He addressed Carolina directly with his final statement. She shook her head slightly before releasing a barely audible whisper. "I can't fight any more. I just want to live …," She turned to Ben as she gently laid her hand on his arm before finishing her thought. "… while I still can."

§

Carolina regained some of her strength—thanks to the care and pain management provided by Hospice—but scars from her treatments remained.

She stood in front of the mirror, examining the burn marks on her body. Could it really be only nine months ago when life was normal and her body hadn't served as a battlefield for two brutal military units?

During that time, she'd been focused on one thing. Fighting. She had fought for Ben and for Rachael, but now she needed a mindset shift. She didn't have to fight anymore.

Carolina was dying.

She would soon be only a memory for her family and friends while she sang praise songs before God. Until then, she needed to do only one thing—live. Live with the two loves of her life until her time with them was spent. One question gripped her mind.

How can you live when you're dying?

She lifted the most precious memories of her life to the front of her mind. She closed her eyes and recalled Ben's face as he lifted her veil on their wedding day. She saw it again, full of love and tenderness on their wedding night and so many nights after. The trips they took together; the tears they shed as they faced the possibility of a life without children; the joy that accompanied that final pregnancy test. And then, the moments full of smiles shared and fingers clutched in a tiny hand, timid steps and giggling while running. Movie nights with popcorn under blankets and flour-covered afternoons in a balmy kitchen. Memory after memory scrolled through her mind until she opened her eyes to reexamine the scars.

Carolina looked up at the mirror before her to find her husband standing behind her, his smile wistful. Their eyes locked, and he closed the space between them. As he wrapped his arms around the woman he loved more than his own life, he leaned down to tenderly kiss the marks of her warrior spirit.

His kisses filled her with light after her emergence from dark and hazy days. She opened her eyes and smiled as she faced him. "I don't want to miss a moment with you and with Rachael. I'm ready to live the rest of my life with you both. I want to soak up every second like this—of being in your arms, gazing in your ocean eyes, kissing those sexy lips of yours." She winked and then she kissed her husband like she hadn't been able to do for a long while. "I want to embrace this good thing—our life together."

Carolina had answered the question of how to live while she was dying, and she was ready to begin.

Letters for Rachael

~~When You Face Death~~
When You Embrace Life

This seems like an odd letter to write to you, and I hope that so many decades have gone by before you need to open this that the paper is yellowed and brittle. I suppose you may never read this. Many people don't get a warning that the end is near for them. I suppose I could consider myself lucky that I knew it was coming.

These past few months, I have basked in the delight of every moment spent with you and your father. I haven't taken little things for granted like I used to—a kiss hello or goodbye, the sound of your laughter rippling along the breeze as you play catch outside with Daddy. I don't get annoyed at silly things either because, really, who's got time for that? Time is precious, and there's so little of it, why waste it with pettiness and sullenness?

Now that I look back, I wish I'd always lived like I had cancer. How much happier would life have been? What would I have not missed?

Earlier this week, I decided to live. Dr. Kumari told me we could try more treatments, but why? I can barely hold this pen right now. This last round of treatments did far more to kill me than the cancer, that's for sure. Since it continues to spread, I know earthly life past this disease is not possible; so, for the time I have remaining, I choose to live.

Death is nothing to fear, though, my dear. I know Jesus, my Savior, will greet me with open arms. He will welcome me to eternity with him where I will never hurt again. I will never be tired again, and my body will never again be simultaneously attacked from the inside and outside. There will be no more death, no more sorrow. And, one day, perhaps soon after you're reading this, I will hold you in my arms again, my beautiful baby girl.

I suppose there's really not much to say about facing death. It's nothing to fear. All your loved ones who also serve God will see you again, so you're not really saying goodbye. So, instead of "When You Face Death," how about I rename this, "When You Embrace Life"?

Take every opportunity you have to say "I love you," to share God's word, to hug your loved ones longer. Enjoy the small moments; don't overlook them in the busyness, for they are the gems in the mines of life. Take time to stop and help or even just smile. Call up a friend you haven't seen in a while just to say hi and catch up.

Ignore the petty things that threaten to fire up that redhead temper I passed on to you. See all the sunsets and sunrises you can, preferably with someone special. Always stop to admire a rainbow—don't take them for granted.

Take some chances, especially when it comes to your dreams and what you're passionate about. If you have an okay job but it's not your passion, step out on faith and find a way to combine your passion with a job. And, most of all, live for Jesus. Show his love to all you meet and honor him in all you do.

Well, this letter went a different direction. Perhaps you should read this as far removed from the end of your life as possible. How much better could life be if we all lived with an ever-present reminder that death comes with the blink of an eye?

VIII

Smelling Blossoms

"Mama, could you teach me how to French braid my own hair?" Rachael's voice sounded small as she snuggled against her mother on their couch one Friday morning.

Her daughter's request squeezed Carolina's heart. She draped her arm around Rachael's shoulders and pulled her closer as she kissed her head. "I would love to, Sunflower."

Rachael looked up and smiled. "Actually, a braiding lesson can wait. It's kind of nice to just snuggle."

"I agree." Carolina held her daughter tightly as she breathed in the vanilla scent of Rachael's favorite shampoo. She smiled at the memory of nine-year-old Rachael declaring herself too old for "kid" shampoo. They had spent twenty minutes on the haircare aisle while she sniffed each bottle at least once.

"Mama?" Carolina nodded against her daughter's head. "This is so hard. I'm trying to be okay, but … I love you. I don't want to say goodbye." Rachael's sobs hit hard.

"Oh, my beautiful girl, I don't either." Carolina pulled her daughter to her heart as they cried themselves out together. Once stillness returned, she continued. "You do not have to be okay. Nothing about this insanity is okay. This isn't the way I envisioned my life, that's for sure. It's okay to be sad—even mad. Don't bury any of these emotions. God gave us emotions as a release, a way to sort through the confusion swirling around us; then his peace and comfort help us emerge from the sea of feelings and not be held captive by them. Remember Daddy's sermon about the Psalms back before Christmas … when the flu was so bad? We listened to it on tape since we had to miss that week."

Rachael nodded as she reached for another tissue.

Carolina smoothed her daughter's hair. "We can still cry together and laugh together and pray together and make memories together. We'll do those things for as long as I have. And, one day, you will laugh and make your own memories. And, that's wonderful."

"I keep thinking of all the things you won't … won't be here for," Rachael spoke between sniffs. "… and I get so sad. And mad too. What will I do without you? Who will I ask all my questions? Who will I tell my secrets? And—another thing—I don't want to laugh and make memories … without you."

"You'll still have Daddy. I know boys aren't quite as good at secrets and girly questions, but give him a shot. I guarantee he'll be way better at them than you think."

"I can try, but I have a feeling there will be some girl things Daddy can't handle." Rachael shook her head, clearly unconvinced with the arrangements.

Carolina laughed. "Well, don't worry; I'm not done. Ms. Becky is pretty amazing, and she's told me she would be happy to answer any questions you have or be there if you just want to have a girls' day." She leaned closer to her daughter before whispering, "Between you and me, I think she'd love to have someone to paint nails with, and Jack doesn't seem too willing."

Rachael crinkled her nose and belly laughed at the thought of her closest guy friend painting his nails.

"As for your not wanting to laugh and make memories without me—baby girl, the thought of you not doing those things breaks my heart. I want you to live a joy-filled life with great friends and incredible experiences."

Carolina sat straighter, facing her daughter, as she brushed the hair from Rachael's face, her hands resting on her cheeks. "You're going to have wonderful, beautiful girl friends who come into your life. The closest and best and truest of those will be with you through life. They're the ones you can confide in and turn to. Choose friends who love Jesus and follow him, and you will be able to help each other in mighty ways as you go through this crazy journey of life."

Mother and daughter sat facing one another, hands together, as Carolina continued. "Better than all, though, Rach, you have God. You can talk to him anytime, anywhere, about anything. He will answer you through the time you spend reading his word and sometimes through the people he puts in your life." Carolina stood up and pulled her daughter with her. "I do have one thing more ... come with me."

They walked hand in hand to the master bedroom where Rachael hopped onto her parents' bed as her mother reached to the top shelf of her closet. Carolina emerged with a cedar box, the size of a shoe box. On the top was a painting in progress; a sunflower had been sketched and outlined with paint. Rachael recognized the color patches in each section of the image as the paints her mother had meticulously selected at a craft store in Atlanta after a draining chemo treatment. As her mother sat beside her and opened the lid, Rachael inhaled the spicy sweetness of the cedar wood.

Carolina looked at the gift in her lap through misty eyes as she tilted the box, nearly full with its contents, toward her daughter. "These are yours. Letters for all the times in your life I can think of when you may want to talk to me or ask something or share something."

She watched the tears splash on her daughter's hands until the little voice she loved to hear spoke. "This is the best gift. Thank you." Rachael examined several of the letters—"When You Have a Job Interview," "When You Start College," "When You Choose a Career," "When You're Having a Bad Day"—and then looked up at her mother, a smile shining through her waterfall.

"Now that you know about it, would you like to help me finish painting? I can't get the shade of yellow for the petals quite right."

"I would love to!"

"We may need some lemonade and cookies first. Can't paint on an empty stomach!" Carolina winked at her daughter.

Rachael cradled her treasure as Carolina gathered the art supplies. They spent the rest of the day eating, finishing the sunflower, painting fingernails, trying various styles on Rachael's hair, talking and adding to their memories.

§

That evening, Ben returned from a pastors' conference to be greeted by his two girls in pajamas with makeup on and nails painted a variety of colors. Rachael's dolls were lined up, each with braided hair. Her own hair was braided—slightly crooked, but braided nonetheless. Carolina sported her favorite red scarf with a fun new bow tied in the front, thanks to Rachael's creativity. Empty popcorn bags and a nearly empty pan of brownies evidenced their impromptu party.

Ben staggered and chuckled as Rachael leapt into his arms for a hug before shimmying down and pulling him after her toward the sofa. She talked as they went. "We've had the best day. Mama taught me to braid my hair. Whaddaya' think?" She twirled around so he could see the back.

"Not bad, Chickadee. Pretty impressive, actually." He smiled at his wife across their daughter's head as she bounced back on the couch between them.

"And, we finished painting this beautiful box." Rachael pointed toward the cedar box on the coffee table. "Did you know Mama's been writing me letters?"

"I did know that." Sorrow surfaced on Ben's face as he hugged his family tighter. "She's a pretty amazing lady."

Rachael looked up at her mother's glowing face and beamed. "She's more than amazing. She's spectacular!"

They ended their night with pizza and *The Sound of Music*. Rachael fell asleep curled up between her parents, so Ben carried her to bed as the credits rolled.

When he returned, Carolina sat as she often did, feet tucked beneath her, one elbow perched on the back of the couch and her temple resting on her fist. She smiled at her husband as he sat facing her.

"Why did it take an invasion of incurable cancer to make me slow down and embrace a day like this?" She gestured around the room to the snack and supper remnants, toys, games, paint supplies—and the splotches that avoided their rushed mop-up following a giggle-induced spill. "This mess is simply a reminder of the uninterrupted time I got to spend with my baby girl and my incredible husband. I love you more today than yesterday."

Carolina whispered the final phrase as she leaned in to kiss him. They made up for the months of not being able to enjoy such a simple action. Remembering that time made each new kiss sweeter. Ben held her lips to his gently, willing all his passion into that touch. As he held the woman of his dreams, he didn't want to lose the sensation of their breaths entwining in an invisible dance of love.

He longed to simply inhale the poison from her body, take it into his own and leave her free and well—healed to live for decades to come. He thought of their near future, the one barreling toward them so much faster than he was prepared to accept; and he wrapped her more completely in his arms. Perhaps if he held her close enough, maybe he could shield her from the inevitable they'd unwillingly accepted.

When they separated for air, he whispered, "You've always been my inspiration. On the hardest days of my life, you've been there. Through addiction, through seminary, through the uncertainty we faced with trying to have a child, through deciding to move to Bellum—you're the one who strengthened me, kept me focused, made me certain. How can I possibly face the absolute hardest day of my entire life ... without my best half?"

"With faith and peace from the One who used me to comfort you in the past. He won't leave you." She framed Ben's damp face in her hands as she held his gaze with her own. "And, I want you to move on. If God brings a new helper into your life, I want you to know I'll be cheering for you both. Don't shake your head at me. I mean it. I don't want you to be alone."

Ben pressed his forehead against his wife's and whispered, "I won't be."

As they clung to one another, sounds of the southern summer night drifted through the window screens. Crickets, katydids and frogs harmonized to serenade them and the love they desired to share as long as earthly possible.

Letters for Rachael

When You Become a Mother

Yesterday—for me, as I'm writing this—you and I spent the day together. You helped me finish painting the sunflower on your cedar box. I never could have gotten that shade of yellow right without you! Thank you for that and for the whole day. What a beautiful gift it was!

I told your father last night how sad I was that it took a monster like cancer to make me slow down and enjoy a busy, messy, silly ... incredible, memory-making day like that with you. As we laughed and played and chatted together, I witnessed your past, present, future and forever.

When I held you as we cried or just snuggled, I remembered how tiny and warm and squishy you felt the first time I held you. I felt so inadequate and also so in love in that moment—those emotions tend to go together often when you're a mom.

I love just being in the moment with you. Too often in your life, I've made myself too busy to focus on the now and pushed it off to then. Problem is, we're never promised then.

As we chatted, I heard your future in the words and dreams and hopes and curiosities you spoke. My darling Rachael, I know you will be kind and loving. You will live a life of passion and unwavering devotion to whatever and whoever God gifts you. You will move mountains, little one, with your fierce drive and determination. You will also move the people around you—in the best possible way. I see how God has gifted you to bring out the best in anyone who lets you into their life for even just a moment.

And, in your heart, I see your forever. My precious daughter—my sister in Christ—I still see your wide blue eyes sparkling on that sunny Sunday when you were only five and you told me you wanted Jesus to be your Lord and Savior so you could live for him alone. There are no more beautiful and precious words than those to a mama's ears. And, in your deep questions about how to live for him and how to share him with others, I see your heart and know your forever lies in the same place as mine—in heaven with our Savior.

So, now—whenever now is—as you prepare to welcome your own little bundle, I know you're excited and nervous and giddy and terrified all at once. I certainly was. Your father and I prayed for a baby. My doctor in Idaho told us it may not be in the cards for us. I cried so hard. I'll never forget that day. After our appointment, Daddy had to go be with a family in our church while they said goodbye to a loved one. I went to some shops to walk around, then a park. Everywhere I went, I saw moms with their kids or ladies who were pregnant. It felt unfair. So, I drove to a resort near Galena Summit. I parked the car and hiked for a while, not really paying attention to where I was or what was around me. After stumbling around for a while—it's hard to walk when you're crying too hard to see—I collapsed onto a fallen tree.

Once my tears were spent, I finally saw around me. The grass looked more vibrant green than I'd ever seen. I noticed colorful flowers wherever I looked. Butterflies and dragonflies fluttered graceful dances all around the valley ahead of me, and my eyes were drawn straight up the mountain before me. As I looked all the way to the tippy-top, a verse came to mind. Remember the one you learned last summer in Bible school about how God *clothes the lilies of the field, even though they don't do anything to make themselves pretty? God provides a way for those humble flowers to be majestic. Such a simple extra; but, if God even cares about the flowers, how much more does he care for us—his children? So, as I looked at the majesty in his creation around me, he filled me with a peace like I'd never felt. I knew— whether he granted my desire or not—I could be content because he would supply every one of my needs. In that moment, the sun glistened brighter off the mountain's peak, and all the colors around me intensified in the most surreal way. I believe that's when my fondness of gardening bloomed into a passion.*

I continued to pray for a child, but I was no longer discontent. When we decided God's plan for us included a move from Idaho to Bellum, I didn't even picture pushing a stroller into the church. It seemed God had other plans. And then, I was expecting you. When you kicked the first time—wow! It was incredible. You did kick hard! I know I felt you much earlier than that, though. Every now and then, I would feel a tiny flutter inside ... like butterfly's wings passing near your face. I marveled when I thought about the tiny life growing inside of me.

I am so happy for you to experience all of these things. I pray health and comfort for your pregnancy— or as much comfort as is possible when you feel like you're walking around with a giant bowling ball resting on your bladder.

The first thing to know about being a mom is there's no instruction manual. You won't know what on earth you're doing the majority of the time. And that's okay. Every child is different; every family is different; every life presents different challenges and trials. The best advice I can give you is to trust your instincts. Every person you meet will give you free and well-meaning (though most often conflicting, more often annoying and rarely requested) "advice." Listen if you'd like and certainly consider more educated tips; but, at the end of the day, you are the mom. You may not always have the answers; but, when you really listen to that voice deep inside, you will find you often do know what's best for your little one.

The next thing I have to share is being a mother is the hardest thing you will ever do. That little bundle of cuteness will demand every ounce of strength you have and then rob you of any rest, demand your undivided attention and require you to anticipate—and fulfill—each and every need and desire. That squirmy mini-you will break your heart, frustrate you and under-appreciate you. But ... you'll experience a tiny fist squeeze your finger, be the recipient of a first smile, hear coos of contentment, watch the pride of first solo steps, accept sticky kisses and fill up a drawer with drawings and cards and random art projects. Just remember, at the end of the day—especially on the rough ones when you lose your temper or feel all alone or think you're the worst mother in the history of mothers—you are not alone. You can do this. God gave you this child, and he gave you every skill and instinct you need to raise, mold and nurture this child.

Just to prepare you for the inevitable, you will fail. Every mother does, but that's okay. You won't mess your child up for life or take a wrong turn you can't come back from. You will have regrets, but don't let them bury you. Learn from them and move forward.

Pray for your child. Give time to your child. Love your child. At the end of the day, the primary desires of every child are to be loved, to be heard, to be taught, to be guided and to be invested in through time, words and deeds.

Drink in every moment and make as many days like our messy, silly, crazy, beautiful one with your little one as you can.

IX

Gathering Harvest

Ben sat on the back porch. A recurring nightmare had woken him and driven him outside. He hoped the fresh air would clear his head. The warmth of the plaid flannel blanket he'd grabbed from the back of their sofa spread through him as the early morning chill bit his nose and cheeks. He pictured the landscape of their yard, still blanketed with night's darkness. He could identify very few of the plants that grew there, but he smiled as he considered how Carolina knew each one's common name, Latin name, characteristics, properties, growth patterns, history and any legends associated with it—and could recite them all while sounding poetic. This yard would never be the same without Carolina tending the plants and caring for the soil. The black expanse before him seemed to have already lost hope and submitted itself to a barren future.

He squeezed his eyes and willed the black thoughts within to disappear. The same nightmare had plagued him for a couple of weeks. In it, he and Carolina walked, hands together, to a train station. They stepped up to board the train, but something entangled him. Carolina climbed the stairs as the train began to glide; but he was caught, unable to follow. Her hand slipped from his as the train ripped her from his grasp. It shot her out of sight before he could even call her name. That's when he would sit up in bed, awake in a cold sweat, his heart knocking violently against his chest.

When he raised his eyelids again, Ben discovered tendrils of light, inching their way across the edges and into the corners of the yard beyond. He knew every midnight eventually met its dawn, but the darkness ahead of him felt impenetrable. A familiar sense of helplessness poured down his body, like an unexpected and unwelcome release of an overhead spout. His beautiful wife faced a great enemy, and he could do nothing. His shoulders slumped as the weight of his inability to heal her or to ease her suffering threatened to crush him.

He pushed his chin up toward the sky as he did the one thing he could and the only thing he should. He prayed.

"Father God, I'm helpless. Carolina is hurting, aching …. God, she's dying … I can't do a single thing to stop it. I'm useless."

Ben paused before continuing. "Every bit of what I just said was focused on me—again. Lord, I do want to be there for Carolina, to support and help and love and comfort however I can. Show me how to help. Keep my mind focused on the time we have left and the sweet moments we get to share. Thank you for the incredible woman you gifted me—for her boundless love and the opportunity I've had to love her. I know you created her for me and me for her, and I thank you for the fit our life together has been … and will continue to be."

He lowered his head and opened his eyes, focusing upon the center flower bed. The waking sun lit up Carolina's dream roses like a wildfire preserved in a snapshot. He may never know as much as Carolina did about all these plants, despite all she'd taught him over the past several weeks, but he could listen to everything that beloved plant had to tell him. He would make sure those roses continued to bloom long after his wife was gone. That was one small thing he could do for her.

§

Carolina smiled at the picture framed in their French doors—Ben with a sunrise halo. This used to be her favorite time of day. She loved the cleansing dew and the newness as everything came awake to face a fresh day under God's brilliant expanse. She'd been sleeping so late that she hadn't enjoyed this splendor for too long.

Ben turned as she walked out to join him. He was more handsome to her in that moment than on the first day they met. They shared smiles, and she sat in his lap to snuggle against his chest. He pulled her warmth into himself as he wrapped her in his arms. Her contentment spoke in a sigh as they watched the brilliance of her dream rose grow brighter with every move of the sun's glow.

"I may not be able to keep your garden exactly how you made it, but I will keep your rose alive for you."

Carolina rewarded his whispered promise with a kiss. "Thank you."

As he stroked her arm, Ben spoke. "I'm sorry for not being stronger for you."

Carolina heard the tears in his tone and longed to comfort him, but he held her close to his chest as he continued. "I don't want to lose you. I want to keep you here with me. It's selfish and flies in the face of the faith I claim; but I've been praying, asking God to help me. You've been so strong; so faithful. I need to be leading you, not sitting here thinking only of myself and my pain."

Once Ben finished speaking, Carolina sat up to face him. She cupped his damp cheek and smiled before feathering a kiss on his lips. "You don't owe me an apology. I have felt all the same things. But, this is harder now for you."

She laughed at the confusion on her husband's face. "Once I ended treatments, I had to figure out how to simply live, not fight or work toward some impossible hope. After God showed me how to do that, he kept instructing me. See, I held on to anger that I had to miss out on our future. The thing is, though, you're not my ultimate future. Whether we have twenty-five years of love or a hundred, God is still my final future. He is who holds my eternity, not you."

Her smile rivaled the rose's brilliance as she continued. "You and I will be together again, but it will be in our eternity with our Creator. The reason this is easier for me is my eternity's coming soon. And, it's going to be more beautiful than anything I could ever dream. But you— you have to finish your life. Yes, live it for our daughter, for the people of Bellum; but none of them are your ultimate future either. That will come one day, most likely a long time from now. Whenever it is, though, it won't feel long to me."

Ben's eyes shimmered with emotion as he gently brushed his wife's lips with his thumb. "God blessed me with you. Thank you for sharing your wisdom, and thank you for loving me in my good and bad, strength and weakness."

"Always."

§

Carolina weakened as the summer heated up. Though her pain was mostly managed, her exhaustion remained. More often, simple tasks left her gulping for air. She continued Rachael's cooking lessons from her chair. Their laughter and chatter continued despite her fatigue. One special night, Carolina instructed Rachael to make Ben's favorite—

homemade spaghetti and meatballs. He was a simple man and declared only Carolina's homemade sauce and meatballs would do. She had been saving this cooking lesson for their sixteenth wedding anniversary.

Rachael learned her lesson well, and Carolina declared it better than she'd ever made. Rachael set the table for two, despite her mother's protests, and lit candles before taking her own dinner to her room.

Carolina and Ben reminisced about each anniversary they'd celebrated, from the first spent hiking in the Rockies to the trip to California the next, in a moving truck the third and sleep-deprived with a newborn on their fourth. From that year on, Rachael had shared in their special dinners ... until that year when their wise girl knew they needed to be alone.

Ben put away their dishes when he saw Carolina fading beneath her weariness. He lifted his bride in his arms as she rested her head against his shoulder, a smile on her lips, and carried her to their bed. That night would be all about holding her tightly as she slept and thanking God for one final chance to celebrate the gift of their marriage.

§

True to her word, Becky had brought Jack with her to help Carolina realize her final gardening vision. They had created and tilled and prepared five rows on the west side of the Burns' house, exactly as she had requested. When they asked what she was going to plant, she answered, "You'll see. It will be a surprise for all of you."

The August sun beat down on Carolina as she knelt beside the fifth row, her breathing labored. Becky had insisted on being with her and holding an umbrella over her for shade each time she planted. This was the final session.

With each seed Carolina nestled into the earth's womb, she said another prayer for the people she was leaving behind as she summoned a much-needed deeper breath.

Plop.

Inhale.

May Rachael grow strong in her faith.

Exhale.

Pat. Pat.

Plop.

Inhale.

Grant Ben wisdom as he seeks your guidance for his future.

Exhale.

Pat. Pat.

Plop.

Inhale.

Comfort my family when I come home to you.

Exhale.

Pat. Pat.

Letters for Rachael

When You Need to Grieve

It's okay to cry. It's okay to not be okay. It's not okay to hold all your emotions in and away from the people God puts in your life to guide you, walk beside you and love you.

That's what I did at the beginning of my diagnosis—hold it deep inside. I didn't want anyone to see my fear, my sadness, my pain. I thought it would be selfish to let others see all that. Turns out, I was wrong.

One night soon after we got the news, your father found me, hiding in our closet and attempting to bawl quietly. It was the first time I'd let myself cry since the diagnosis. At first I felt so horribly selfish that he had witnessed my breakdown. Then I saw my pain and anguish mirrored in his face as he started to cry. He dropped to his knees and wrapped his arms around my shaking shoulders.

"Thank God!" he whispered. I had no idea why he was thanking God for finding me crumpled and crying on our closet floor and so I cried harder … this time with him. Later, he helped me understand that he needed to share his grief and hurt and anger with me but didn't think he could. All he had seen was the cheerful, positive mask I'd been wearing.

Turns out, grieving together was exactly what we both needed. So, baby girl, you can cry. You can share your emotions—good or bad. You can share with Daddy and with your closest friends, the ones you know God's sent you to be your special people. Of course, you can cry out to God because he is always listening, and he cares about everything in your life. You are his princess, and he loves you.

Plus, you can share them with me. I may not be right here beside you, but I'll be waiting for you in heaven. You can feel my presence in your heart. I will always be your mama who loves you and wants to hear your joys, your hurts, your sorrows, your frustration, your everything.

I love you, my beautiful sunflower, and I always will. You cry, share, talk ... any time. Let it out. Grieve.

X

Resting Earth

Birds rose slowly that morning—like they didn't want to venture away from night's protective blanket. Ben's eyes shied from the sun's rays. He slid his arm gently across Carolina's waist, his heart dropping as he brushed against her jutting hip bones.

Her breathing felt too shallow. He thought his heart disappeared altogether as the realization sprung his eyelids free of slumber's chains. Her eyes—those deep emerald pools of wisdom and empathy—rested open. He could tell she'd been awake for a while. Why hadn't she woken him? He craved every moment he could cherish with her.

A hint of a smile touched the corners of her lips as she spoke.

"Mornin', sleepyhead." He heard the breathless pain and dryness in her voice. He also heard her endless love and longing for more.

More time. More good mornings. More afternoons at the lake with her husband and daughter. More peaceful moments hand in hand on the porch. More seasons of careful tilling, planting, pruning and watering.

More.

Ben raised himself on an elbow to look down into the face that had been his constant, his guide, his beacon in all he was called to be and do. From somewhere in the reserves of his breaking heart, he pulled a smile—the kind his gorgeous wife deserved.

"Good morning, beautiful." Her smile's hint grew more certain. He knew she loved that greeting. Even with the patches of scalp showing through her thinned, fiery hair that had only recently begun to regrow and the radiation burns peeking beneath the straps of her gown, Ben meant that word, and he needed her to know it.

Ben kissed the tear that spilled from the corner of her eye before he nodded to the marked calendar. The first two days' boxes held bright red hearts. Around the third was a thick red box.

"God gave us twenty-five years together, plus one year more."

Too weak to nod, her tired eyes still danced in agreement. She worked her eyelids and throat, begging her body for a hint of relieving moisture. Eyes still closed, she opened her mouth and whispered, "It's time. You made this life worth it all. I love you more today ... than all our yesterdays."

Her eyes fought open as they rained down her parched face. "I will see you soon ... in our ever more."

Ben's emotion mingled with hers as he caressed her cheek and tenderly held one slender hand in his. "You will forever be my one, my beautiful Carolina. Go to Jesus—to relief from your pain. I'll meet you when my journey here is done."

Her smile shone as peace and relief flooded her freed soul and failed body.

"Love our girl. I love you both ... eternally."

A breeze rustled their curtains as it ushered in the trill of a whip-poor-will.

Epilogue

Just over a week had passed since they laid Carolina to rest in the earth she loved. Ben walked onto their deck as the sun rose higher in the sky. He needed to leave for the church. Maybe he wasn't ready to preach so soon. Nothing felt right without his wife by his side.

As an internal war waged, he leaned against the rail. He had almost decided to call one of the deacons and explain he simply wasn't ready when something caught his eye. His breath caught in his chest. He went back inside.

Rachael stood by the kitchen sink, an untouched glass of milk leaning in her hand as she stared at nothing out the window. Ben walked to her, set her glass down and took her empty hand. He led her outside and pointed west, where the first row of sunflowers was rising to greet the glow above.

§

A gust of wind whooshed around Rachael, reminding her that winter had arrived. Thanksgiving wouldn't be the same without her mom. She had baked the pies and made all her mom's favorite dishes. Her dad was in the kitchen fussing over the turkey, and Ms. Becky was on the way with a trunk load of food.

Before the house filled up, though, she needed fresh air. She walked to her mother's final masterpiece. Every week for five weeks, a new row of sunflowers had bloomed. Somehow, a few blossoms still clung to their stalks. She knew enough about flowers to know this wasn't typical sunflower behavior. The last few towered above Rachael. As she looked up at them, a cloud parted and the sun caressed her cheeks.

She closed her eyes and laughed.

"I love you, Mama."

Acknowledgments

Behind each book I produce, I have an army of supporters who helped make it happen. *This Good Thing* is no different.

Though I don't deserve *any good thing,* GOD has gifted me *this good thing* and granted me the ability to tell stories while I live it.

To TONY, I love you more today than yesterday.

To ALLIE, thank you for inspiring the heart of Carolina's story.

To RACHAEL RITCHEY, your design never ceases to amaze me. Thank you for believing in my work and for making it shine.

To my critique partners, though none of you got to read this before it was cast into the world, you each played a role in making it happen. DEVON HARRY, KELSEY ATKINS and TAURI COX, thanks for the encouragement when I sent out my mess of an outline during that long-ago Camp NaNo. MEA SMITH, thank you for encouraging me to keep going and for loving Carolina with me. Also, Becky thanks you for her voice.

Though this story is fiction, it was imperative that I put as much fact in it as possible.

Without the help of MARY TRIZILA, RN OCN, I would still be lost in the darkness of cancer treatments. Thank you for shining the light for me and for shining an even more important light for your patients. Thank you to my fellow Writer Mom, LAURA SHIFF, for introducing us.

Fellow Ninja, JOCELYN LINDSAY, you helped the lady who once killed a cactus write about an elaborate garden. Thank you!

To MELANIE PARISH (another sneaky Ninja), for getting me started on the right research path for cancer treatments.

To KELSEY ATKINS, for making me love Idaho from afar.

Without the characters who built this story and the readers who've come to love them, none of us would be here.

To MARY LOU who requested this book every time she saw me after I teased her with the first chapter. I hope it was worth the wait! Thank you for believing in my books.

To my READERS, you are why.

To my church family at NORTHSIDE BAPTIST CHURCH, you're a shining example of how to support a creative. Thank you!

Meet the Author

Photo: Casie Jones Photography

Legacy and identity, founded on hope-filled faith, infuse the tales of the soul written from the heart of JOY E. RANCATORE. Her Carolina's Legacy Collection embraces everyday moments that constitute a lifetime and its heritage. Told around multiple related characters, this collection explores faith, life, death and the demons within through four mediums—novel, novella, short stories and epistolary.

An avid reader, student of human behaviors and unwitting empath, Joy absorbs emotions and spills them onto the pages of her work. Joy's technical background includes more than two decades of professional writing and editing. Ongoing training in writing, publishing, business and counseling enables her to package soul-filled stories for her readers. An award-winning, multi-genre Indie Author, Joy believes extraordinary things await her characters and their tales.

Despite a fondness for her roles as author, editor, podcaster and speaker, Joy is a hobbit at heart with Bilbo's zeal for mountains. She enjoys a life of quiet stillness with her husband, two children, dog and cat and more books than she's willing to count. When daily homeschool lessons are complete, she eagerly prepares for teatime before writing your next favorite story.

Visit Joy for Book News, Free Stories, Book Club Kits and More:
www.joyerancatore.com/links

Have a Book Club?

READ:

Any Good Thing
(or any book in Carolina's Legacy Collection)
together.

REQUEST:

- a Book Club Kit
- a virtual or in-person chat with the author

VISIT:

www.joyerancatore.com/book-clubs

Did You Enjoy This Book?

Reviews from readers make the most precious gift for authors and help fellow readers discover fantastic new reads. Please take a moment to leave a simple star review or a few thoughts on Goodreads and any bookseller sites.

Another way to share your appreciation is to tell all your reader friends and request that your local bookstore and library shelve it.

Share your reviews and book selfies with Joy and Logos & Mythos Press on your favorite social media outlets. #ThisGoodThing

Colophon

The typeface used with gracious permission in the cover design and throughout the book is Bentham, created by designer and developer, Ben Weiner. Interior formatting is primarily 11 point sizing. Subeadings fluctuate between 16 and 24 point sizing. For more on this typeface, read the creator's description:

"I like the lettering on nineteenth-century maps, on gravestones and on the maker's plates of cast-iron machinery. It is characterised by expressive flowing and bulging curves, mannered awkwardness and the bobbles on the terminals of its characters. The letterform conventionally called 'modern face' is the typographical equivalent, and it can be found in books printed throughout the nineteenth century. Its descendants survived into educational textbooks produced into the late twentieth century, and it is preserved in computer science as the style which Donald Knuth adopted for his TEX typesetting system.

"Bentham is a half-way design; it's true neither to the type produced during the nineteenth century, nor to the letterforms of cartographers, stonecutters, or engravers. It's really a sort of examination of the characteristics these letters share, coloured by my approach to type drawing."

Headings formatted throughout the book are Allura font in primarily 26 to 36 point sizing. Allura is the script format of the Allura Pro family. Like other designs by Rob Leuschke, Allura is stylized, yet very legible.

Want More?

For more information on upcoming releases from
LOGOS & MYTHOS PRESS

Visit logosandmythospress.com/links and subscribe to their
email list.

Thank you for reading!

LOGOS & MYTHOS PRESS
SLIDELL, LA, USA